Eagle and th' Fiv' Eggs

A Work of Modern Literature

MS Firdaus (IFW.104)

(A Theatrical Play Masterpiece)

Eagle and th' Five Eggs

Contents

Note: This is an interactive PDF. Instructions to navigate are as of the followings:

(a) Click the content's headings to go to pages.

(b) Click to go for reference. And click <XX) to return to the same page before.

(c) Click [S.xx] for song's references. And click <XX) to return to the same page before.

(d) Click (F.xx) for French meaning in English. And click <XX) to return to the same page before.

A Work of Modern Literature

By Muhammad Firdaus Sidek of
Ido Firadyanié Art Nouveau (iFAN Music & Art)
Note: Previously sobriquet by Ido Firadyanie Marcolini, hence by the release of iFAN 1st Music Album 'Rhythm in the Night', Ido Firadyanie has hence changed to Ido Firadyanié Art Nouveau
[ISNIcode:0000000491304973]

His real name as what stated in his NRIC/IC is Muhammad Firdaus bin Sidek. This masterpiece was written at Kampung Bukit Kuari, 86400 Pos Parit Raja, Batu Pahat, Johore, Peninsular Malaysia.

THE PLOT

Eagle and th' Fiv' Eggs
(5 Acts Comically Operatic Play/Film)

PART I
(ACTS I, II & III)

ACT I

I. Scene I – This dreamt fable starts with Caesarea, just finishing his 'door to door' business. In a brief suddenness, he is alarmed by a cry from a parked car (an Estima estate van). He nears and encounters a woman (Solania), whom is close to 'bring forth' her baby. While doubtful of self-stalwartness, he aids her; but, is then astonished by the anomalous production — the five eggs. Whereby Solania has already fainted. Edgily licenseless and inexperience at driving, he tries to steer the car — sending her to hospital. Insensibly an obstacle, he is blocked by a roadblock.

I. Scene II – An RTD/JPJ officer and a Sikh traffic police have made known from Caesarea's identification and clarification for 'driving without license'; and Caesarea is summoned. But as deliberation is confirmed upon Caesarea's reason for every of his action, the RTD officer reduces the fine. Still in indisposition, Caesarea has drawn a bargain; but agreeable with the demand of the law, nevertheless, he accepts the stated amount. He continues his course.

I. Scene III – Passes two Chinese nurses, within the scenario in the University Hospital (PPUM, Petaling Jaya), grumbling about their occupation. Hence, shifting into one of the rooms, Caesarea is attending Solania; of whom has just regained her consciousness. They spend a conversation of which has enlivened exchanges of self-introduction and appreciations amongst themselves. The conversation ends with Caesarea, excusing himself to leave for his hometown — as the reason. And, has promised Solania to visit her again.

I. Scene IV – While waiting for a minibus, Caesarea busies himself, counting a wad of money (Solania's gift of appreciation). He proceeds to the city, thereafter; taking his breakfast and advancing towards the Dangwangi Police Station.

I. Scene V – He settles the fine and travels homeward to Malacca with an express bus.

ACT II

II. Scene I – (A, B & C) – Caesarea reaches his house. Explaining his one day lateness to his mother (Ljiljana); along the experiences with Solania, the five eggs and the benefits in his favour ~ compendiously. Ljiljana accentuates her sympathy and plans with Caesarea to accompany and tend Solania. Concentric with the intrinsic solicitousness, they go and visit Solania.

II. Scene II – Solania is pleased with their arrival. Caesarea's jokes, Ljiljana's evangelical advice, and Solania's gladness are poured in a spirited conversation. Within, Solania has wished them to stay with her and they have agreed, open-heartedly. Because Solania is still insufficient to be released from her medical period, she has therefore recommended Caesarea and Ljiljana to take care of her house. Again, illegally a drive with the Estima, Caesarea and Ljiljana proceed to Solania's dwelling.

II. Scene III – Caesarea begins making his acquaintance with the surroundings of Solania's bungalow, exterior and interior. More than somewhat, a piece of short poem and a portrait (of Jannequin), have advanced a discussion between Ljiljana and Caesarea; amidst their delight on the intriguing wonderment, observed.

II. Scene IV – Solania is released a month thereafter but yet, unrecovered. Despite her illness, she still could describe to them about the history of the five eggs with the portrait of Jannequin as the major connexion.

ACT III

III. Scene I – Solania's first meeting with Jannequin is as a lawyer; studying his hopeless situation as an accused murderer. Comprehensible with his disfavoured case, of which a rejection by 'six advocates' as undefensible, complaisantly she has agreed to defend him. In accordance to Jannequin's lengthy description about his mishap, Solania ascertains the prospect of the case; appraising the strong and the weak points of his stand. Ahead the dispersion of their meeting, Solania is growing to have an interest in him.

III. Scene II (A) – Passing by an interval, it has been the fourth day of the trial. Solania tries to soothe Jannequin before the continuation of the hearing. The humorously judge opens the court, requesting Solania to forward her defence's material. From contributary post-mortems and the previous statements of Jannequin, Solania details the murder of Yvon Laurel by assumption.

III. Scene II (B) – The scene is shifted to Yvon Laurel's apartment at Pandan Indah. Quarelling with Ravioli (the conspirator of the murder), in her dislike to continue their relation as intimate lovers. Infuriated by Yvon's vulgarity, Ravioli provokes to kill her.

III. Scene II (C) – Yvon is finally trapped in the truth of Ravioli's provocation; and, she is victimised in an indecent assault by Ravioli and his five friends/accomplices, at Jalan Stonor, Ampang. During a struggle to shout for help, impulsively Yvon is shot to death.

III. Scene II (D) – Earlier, Ravioli has chummed with Jannequin. Taking advantange of this friendship, Ravioli captures Jannequin as 'his prey'; leaving Jannequin unawarely to survive the consequence of the killing.

III. Scene II (E) – Back in the court, the prosecutor lights a disagreement by taking several views. This lengthens the discord between the prosecutor and Solania until the judge postpones the trial to the next day.

III. Scene III – The hearing of Jannequin's case is heated with the arrival of witnesses. Because of the inadequately statements to prove his being guilty, the judge has thereby approved an assertion of bail made for Jannequin.

III. Scene IV – Solania and Jannequin celebrate the primary win on 'their first date'. Thereof, generating their love; with Jannequin, giving away promises and gifts of five emeralds to Solania.

III. Scene V (A, B & C) – Interval is again elapsed; bringing the trial to its twentieth day. Again, Jannequin has lost hope on his case for the 'assurances made by the witnesses for the prosecution'. Luckily, the existence of Marzipan, Bahrin and Gerard as the 'genuine spectators' of the crime, has confirmed the rightness of Jannequin. Thus brings to the dismissal of the case.

III. Scene VI – Following on the success, it leads both Jannequin and Solania to their marriage. The bungalow, the car (the Estima) and Jannequin's business are given as wedding presents to Solania. But, mischance makes a mockery of their happiness, where, Jannequin returns to his actual existence'— an ordinary eagle. Shifting to Solania's grievance, he has left her forever — 'a human'.

THE PLOT

PART II
(ACTS IV & V)

ACT IV

IV. Scene I – Solania sheds in her grief on Ljiljana's laps. Conscientiously, Caesarea tries to tend Solania. Later on, to his consciousness, he hears chirps from bird's youngs. He runs upstairs into one of the rooms of which he had left the five eggs earlier; and to his delight, all the eggs have hatched. Gladly, he jokes and vociferates with the foundation. Inconsequentially, Solania has acted aloof.

IV. Scene II – Here, Caesarea meets with his customer's wife, Siti Jana; while enlarging a parrot's cage for the five eaglets. Caesarea is pleased with Siti Jana as his close neighbour. Followingly, a postman comes, bringing letters; and astonishingly, one of them is from Jannequin. In the content, Jannequin has beseeched Solania to name the eaglets — Solace, Lovepress, Amethyst, Nixloath and Antidoubt.

This sudden message has agonised Solania's contemporary condition. Before going insensible, she has asked Caesarea to add behind the names — Solace The Compass, Lovepress The West, Amethyst The East, Nixloath The North, and Antidoubt The South. Doctor Alex Tan, (supposedly to be Solania's personal doctor), is called. A rankled answer from the treatment, unfortunately, Solania's disease is deemed cureless and could only await her death. Alternatively, the doctor has prescribed a traditional doctor, Haji Omar, to help curing Solania.

IV. Scene III – Though a well-known medicine man, but Haji Omar has failed to heal Solania.

IV. Scene IV – The medicine man departs. Solania spends her 'final talk' with Caesarea; requesting him to read the 'statements and bequest'. Solania dies on Caesarea's embrace; binding himself and Ljiljana in sorrow.

IV. Scene V – Obeying the instructions as in the letter of concern, Solania is dressed in her wedding gown, and, has been placed at the veranda. 'As midnight calls', Caesarea yells to the sky, urging the eagle's (Jannequin's formation) arrival. The eagle shows up itself and takes Solania's dead body away with it; of which has drawn Caesarea and Ljiljana, dumbfoundedly in between their tears.

IV. Scene VI – On the same night after the tragedy, all the five grown eaglets have strangely transformed themselves into teenagers of three boys and two girls.

IV. Scene VII – Caesarea and Ljiljana are overawed by the emergence of the five youngsters. Overtly overjoyed, they share their love with the children.

IV. Scene VIII – Acting themselves as father and grandmother to the children, Caesarea begins to name them— equally with Solania's previous wish. Whereby, the five emeralds (of which have been set in gold necklaces) are given to the children throughout the naming.

ACT V

V. Scene I – A great interval is passed; changing the appearances of all the previous characters. Lovepress is now has grown up a mature lady. Flying home from London with the British Airways aircraft, she is hence a scholar from Stamford University.

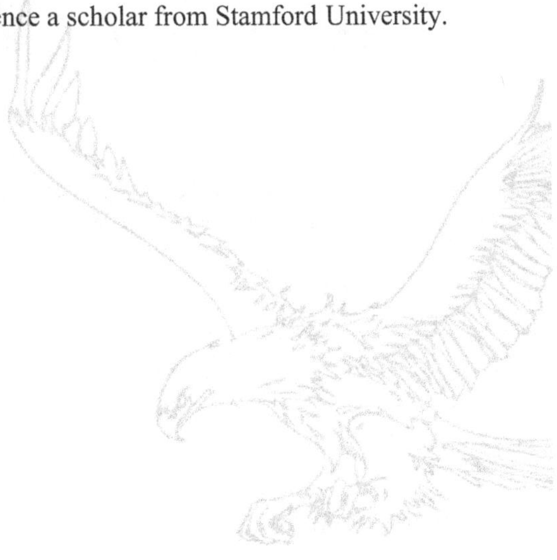

V. Scene II – Shifting the scene to Ampang, two eagles have just transformed themselves into two 'classic rockers' — Nixloath and Antidoubt. Falling in 'everyday conflict' amongst themselves, has brought their time close for Lovepress' party at the family hotel — Concorde, Kuala Lumpur.

V. Scene III – The mid-age Caesarea and old Ljiljana celebrate Lovepress' graduation with all the children, in the '***fashionable private party***'.

DRAMATIST PERSONAE

(Scenes in Selangor, Kuala Lumpur and Malacca)

Caesarea Solania
Ljiljana (Caesarea's mother)
Jannequin [spelt Phillip' for Phillipe Jannequin]
Solace The Compass (I & II)
Lovepress The West (I & II)
Amethyst The East (I & II)
Nixloath The North (I & II)
Antidoubt The South (I & II)
RTD/JPJ Officer (RTD = Road and Transport Department)
Sikh Traffic Police
Hokkien Nurses (I) & (II)
Police Clerk
Policeman
Doctor
Staff Nurse
Malay Nurse Policewoman (Constable)
Judge
Prosecutor
Yvon Laurel
Ravioli
Oxenville (Ravioli's friend/Accomplice I)
Hussein (Ravioli's friend/Accomplice II)
Brown (Witness I)
Bartender (Witness II)
Businessman (Witness III)
Hairdresser (Witness IV)
Cambodian Journalist (Witness V)

Madeina (Witness VI)
Marzipan (Witness VII)
Bahrin (Witness VIII)
Gerard (Witness IX)
Journalists (I) & (II)
Siti Jana (Mr Ashraf's wife)
Postman
Dr Alex Tan (Solania's personal doctor)
Haji Omar (Shaman/Medicine Man)
Traveller
Amy (Antidoubt's Fiancee)
Mohan (Restaurant Manager)
Lee (Restaurant Supervisor)
Lorraine (Waiter's Captain)
Chef Lombardo

Extras: Narrators (Choir of 10 Singers); Mr Ashraf (description); DSP Zaid (description); Spectators (of the trial); A woman spectator and a punk boy (spectators of the trial)

Published by: Ifan Music & Art (Publisher ID: 967-26639)
Address: IFAN MUSIC AND ART, NO. 8, LORONG 8, TONGKANG PECHAH, 83010, BATU PAHAT, JOHORE, MALAYSIA.
TEL.: +6012-6324529

Part I
(ACTS I, II & III)

(This division is for the convenience of actors to memorise the long verses for staged opera, TV Opera, or long Play Film.

- Firadyanié 1998)

Eagle and th' Fiv' Eggs

(5 Acts Comically Operatic Play/Film)
(W.104 of Ido Firadyanié Art Nouveau Collections)

ACT I

Scene I (Tun Dr Ismail Garden, Damansara)

erspire courses Caesarea's forehead. An attempt to succeed the sale, does not knock his head twice against a brick wall – that evening. The uniquely design'd tablecloths as what a carbon copy of his sweatshirt are all sold. Closing his business early at dusk with high profit obtain'd from Mr Ashraf and his wife is by dint of great opportunity for future trade. Howsoe'er, Mr Ashraf 's impressive semi-detach'd bungalow has been twelve-steps away from him. Mr Ashraf 's invitation for Caesarea to have a one night stay at his house after dinner has been refused. And to Caesarea's best reason for his disagreement —

Caesarea: "My mater hath fatherly counselled,
If naught turns nasty and obstacleless,
All th' journeys should be within but two days.
And, I have borne them all deadly serious."

(***But the memory of his deadpan humour has finally come to its disappearance; like fleeing away, when he hears a weep, coming out from a parked Toyota Estima***)

1). Dialogue

Solanla: "O! 'Tis getting pain...
God! My dearest Lord, pray send,
Prithee send someone to me,
I'm urging for a help.
O! Cry no cure, harm no kill,
I couldn't bear this e'ermore."

(*Cries her; voice faint-heartedly*)

Caesarea: "I' to a fool and loon,
This could be a sorely beg from fallen fern,
But for me, she's in the family way.
Whatsoe'er 'tis, i' this famish'dly moment~
Huh! O! God! If said, it is well-nighly
Impossible for me to act wisely
Like a fairy godmother."

(*Disobliges him in dither about the red-paint'd car — either leaving or to help*)

Solanla: "H'm! Hmm!" (*She weeps*)
Am I've been promis'd, O! Am I, Lord?
Risking this exasp'rating suffering?
I am not loath to die rather waiting."

Caesarea: "Felicitating for someone's glory~
Very interesting, while eye's clipping,
List'd but to leave one in adversity,
'Snot quite well-meaning, none the well-meaning.
It is worthier if I behold inside."

(***On the velvet seat, lay a peroxide blonde; swelling belly like a tortoise's shell, legs bent at the knees and is widely opened. Wearing a greyish gown, with pallid aspect, Solania keeps scratching the soft surface — battling against death while panting towards breathless. Caesarea has banter'd near cramps***)

"If there's a balm for this conundrum,
Verily I'm in the need of it, Lord.
Thee, sweet lady; if I'm to be the base o' aids,
Throwst a contemptuous look thou never,
Prithee!"

(***Manfully he calls out:***)

"Hallo?! May I offer a hand?
I' thou'rt set at naught or finically said,
Nor panic-stricken?"

Solania: "Wherefore should I quail?
Sure thou mayst." (***Responds her in brevity***)

Caesarea: "But utter I must; not to lie,
But much not to trust, I'm a proper charlie,
Neither a physician nor a charlatan."

Solania: "Belabour not my pain with thy frolicsome verse,
But shouldn't begone tho' horrid i' th' observation,
But try an effort thyself; galore thy lanterns,
To banish this merciless suffer I burthen."

Caesarea: "I shall try, as thy quota."
(***He opens the door and vaults in***)
"I'm cherishing th' hope,
E'en i' th' minute of chance, well-nigh justly than mischance."

(***Thoroughly he studies Solania while holding her fingers firmly***)

"Thou shouldst be afar from this despondency,
In this helpless place and yet amidst sequester'd,
Unto doom thou'rt deuc'd.
(***Enquires Caesarea in mere civility***)
"Art thou betwixt bearable,
Till I drive this excellent car
To the adjacent hospital?"

Solania: "Naaay!
Not e'en lest perchance, 'tis a vain attempt,
In another brevity, either dead...
(***She pauses with eyes glazing in perspiration***)
"Or quick, my babe may be born to earth."

Caesarea: "Lady, end thy worry.
Pacify thyself from conceit o' misrule,
Shall all misadventures bid by farewell,
And forthwith the mirth sits on thy tail."

Solania: "AAAH!"

(***She cries. Blood trickles between h er legs***)

Caesarea: "Ease thyself, comfort thy spirit, lady.
Thou canst make it."

(***He wipes Solania's forehead with his handkerchief. In dodder he tries delivering her baby — but mere bothersomely, focuses nothing***)

Solania: "O! Heaven inward,
Hell issues forth! 'Tis getting at me.. O!"

Caesarea: "Fine, alright. Naught in a tight spot.
(***Responds him a bit timorously***)

"Yea, yea! 'Tis coming,

Ease thyself, engulfing i' thy pain, lady.
Thou canst make it for this heavenly while.

(***Coated with fresh blood, lay five eggs swan-sized, at an alternate birth period of ten minutes each. Solania has swum — unconscious. Mindfulness of the scene, apacely he replaces the eggs into an empty orange-box; palleted***[M1] ***with a cushion. Using a dry green cloth, he mops the stains and blankets Solania with a ready satin bed-spread***)[1]

"Parts from 'Facts o' Life'; natural insistence,
And this very experience indeed
Are the very stuff of my journal,
Tho' seem an aid given short shrift, heed'd,
For minus o' th' essential competence,
I'm vaunting to this miraculous scene.
And thou, asset of sweet; while sweet is quin,[M2]
Shalt hav' a fine pride of a virago,
Being a noble mater to these five eggs
In thy woe.

(***On the driver's seat, inexperienc'dly he tries to accelerate the motorcar. Chugging unto quick, the motorcar, with smooth ignition; Caesarea inhales contentedly***) (2)

"What's exceptionally good,
Tho' a crabchild for this newfangled with hood,
It doeth me unfettered o' tenterhooks,
Whereas nobuild (M3) likes even a lark,
I've e'en a will imagining myself—
A bright spark." (***He smiles alone***)

To Thy Best (S.i)

Sung Verses (Song) [***8 syllables***]
I ain't a rustic nor a clown,
Mollycoddled all the year round,
By fay tales at a lunar eclipse,
Vast of ebullience and esprits

My wish's nay till to th' vanity,
Where't sal'brious livin' ~ my glory, (M4)
Ravish'd by viands' taste forsooth;
Vastly too, my humor good,
But jocosity, made 'bove crud' (M5)

Unto my convenience, function's lesson;
        Meeting someone gracious and confident,
T'night's wonder isn't mine to pant,
        But bow I ere to this parturition
Of legend—at my redeemable stand

Refrain[3]

To this numerous progeny,
        I' my ratiocination on th' brink,
What on this earth wilt thoube,
        But may live 'ther than starveling

Thy mater alike a demigod,
        From potent death hath herself fought,
Without of[M6] her practical thought,
        In this purlieus o' sordidness[M7],
Naught could solace but to stress

Howsoever she's e'en alive,
        Made myself occupied by rest,
Here garner all hope[M8]; earn glowed life,
        Will there be material guest;
Well-spring of chance to thy best

Caesarea: "Oho! No.
Unto my surprise! 'Tis prepar'd so nice,
A roadblock ahead, for driver nay legal license,
'N' here I to skate on thin ice."

Scene II (SS21/64 Road, Damansara) <4)

2). **Dialogue**

JPJ Officer: "A mountebank... this time, eyes dim like to cry,
Would not play any longer on the sly,
Licence, pray." (***Commands him in gruffly voice***)

Caesarea: "Nay, sir. Have not had any.
And I am stultified insistently,
While this is my one primary attempt
To drive a king-like car brand."

JPJ Officer: "Haven't gotten
Brand'd exceptional excuses?"

Caesarea: "Yea, sir.
Certainly, a story within reasons,
Beneath all my peak'd actions."

JPJ Officer: "Boost the good. (M9)
Be not poor-spirited in the reasons,
Playing a coward does not help thyself
If not then rot, the fine in gnawing full.
Move to th' grass verge and be immediately."

Caesarea: "Immediately? Huh! What an eventide tension!
(*Caesarea corners and brakes the motorcar rather fretful. Well-nighly he contrites:*) [5]

"Cheerless[M10] lapidates warmness,
Insalubrious[M10] updates cheerless,
Tensing up grows i' insalubrious[M10],
Unquiet the answer; gnome's class,
Puts unto shuddering carcass,
And that carcass belongs to me, mind you."

Sikh Traffic Police: "Your identification card?"
(*Demands him in Sinhalese English accent with a wan smile*)

Caesarea: "Here's mine."
(*He hands his I.C. — fingers shiver*)

Sikh Traffic Police: "Thou'rt beseeming surround'd with a hefty hurdle[M11],
Prithee, describe."

JPJ Officer: "Yea, yea. Discredit phantasy.
Carry on with thy fluid truly story[M12],
I am in impatience for additions[M12]."

Caesarea:

Verses – *sing as Aria di Portamento* **(S.II)**[*8 syllables*]

Medescri'd this lone car; arear, <6) (M13)
After winning a profit's hip;
From a remote business trip,
And to my accurately ear,
Meheard clear an intensely weep

Wide-awake, mobile I've realis'd,
She was in the parturition,
Helping what I could—gifted wise;
Till, fiv' swan-size eggs laid, precise,
Unto the flinching succession

Neglecting her just; my loath shy,
Perchance I'm 'lone to sympathise,
Unto the derring-do I'd try,
E'en whatsoe'er betide; nay prize,
Acceptance; part kindliness ties (M14)

I expect nay e'en mut'd respect,
From y' officers: Misters Brave Men,
For my this single homely act;
This lady alying the back, (M15)
Wilting, be treat'd by a physician

JPJ Officer: "A stupefying story to muster,
Inclusive stupendous effort."

Sikh Traffic Police: "'Mong hundred pates, <7) (M16)
Petty sums o' condition's immaculate,
Minusing th' amount are generous sorts,
For many vain folks o' gentrification.
You are supposed ~ stouthearted, city man."

JPJ Officer: "Spot words, if plucked, many insinuations,
But joining hands none for grade — a social restorer.
Yea, but this museum piece should be a photocopy
Of the sorts.
(*Unto Caesarea*) "Apropos for th' laudable action,
The guilty tax is hence reduced quarter
From the total — mere fifty ringgits."

Caesarea: "Shouldst
It be another half from the stated amount;
Short budget o' fuel refill."

Sikh Traffic Police: "Thy demand somehow
Does not make any sense unto the law,
Forasmuch driving licenseless's a great offence,
Where I assume this shan't put thee lesser
Or equal i' queer street." (M17)

JPJ Officer: "Further nay question,
Prithee settle 't today or another
At a simple observable police station."
(***He pushes the bill of fine and the I.C. card roughly to Caesarea's palm***)

Caesarea: "I should be thankful for small mercies."

Sikh Traffic Police: "Bear i' thy mind,
Confining thyself unto illegal driving,
If not, thou'rt or mayst shall not late shall not long,
Be dispirited by another discomfort."

(***Replying nothing, Caesarea speeds the motorcar to University Hospital. And has partly born in his mind, the dissuasion of the decently men***)

EXEUNT

Scene III (Interior of the University Hospital)

Hokkien Nurses 1 & 2: *Singing Duet*

I'm A Wage Slave (S.III)

Sung Verses (Song) [***7 syllables***] (<8)

Playing to the gallery, (M18)
Doeth not fructify ayely,
Sat'd my commend'ble standing,
But an oft-neg'tive ending

A jest may not e'en joyous, [5]
But a slip o' measureless meaning,
With grands naught e'en least precious,
But oppressing doubt'd instinct

A jaunty being for a moment,
    Relaxing th' disconcert'd mind,
Joy i' for little wonderment,
    Is lief a worthwhile find

<u>Refrain</u>

I am a wage slave; (We are just wage slaves),
    All tides and times beseem tough,
For my being as a staff;
(For our beings as staff),
    Taking wages cruc'ble 'nough

I am a wage slave; (We are just wage slaves),
    For my being as a nurse;
    (For our beings as nurses),
Aid patients to a state worst-less,
    With addition o' politeness

2 Nurses Exit

(The staidly nurses vanish into the crowds after completing the undesirable melody. In a private room (1st Class Ward), hard by to where the nurses have disappear'd, sits Caesarea on a swivel chair — taking a little unfortunate doze. Beside him, lying on the white blanket'd bed — Solania has yet astir. Clad in a white patient's tunic, awhile with twitching watery brown eyes — she appears pale and merely in vexation. Vex'd by her intricately pain. Though waxen, her visage of natural beauty remain'd: tresses of but dark, slender nose, and fair-lipp'd of a Malay-Dutch woman. She glances at Caesarea with a smile of an elderly sister. Thereupon admiring her scarlet handbag; tightly held on Caesarea's lap. In tendency to know him more profoundly, she touches his right forearm ~ mildly. He is like hitching to wake up and purblindly stares at her — betwixt dream and reality are in blur)

3). **Dialogue**

Caesarea: "Pardon me if I'm winding up
Thus by my ineptly action,
Merely I am yet sensible.
O! Locus. Unto thy knowledge,
I have abode thine impressive
Descendants—bound in a secure box;
Lock'd in thine maroon estate van.
I' I'm advert'd unto my earnest
Ahearing unto th' history
O' these fiv' eggs; gloss the oblong shells,
Like'ble adorable big pearls,
Mayst thou narrate it to me?"

Solania: "Impossib'litiless I shall,
Unnecessarily quite in this while,
Tidied promise: if permissive time tell,
I' my healthy mien hath return'd —
Possible worthwhile."
(***She sighs warmly with a smile and continues***)
"Thou shouldst be as that languid
For thy being waxed fatigue,
Roaring — thou needst viands and drinks,
To restore thy primrose th' mainspring."
(***She ends in a subdued voice***)

Caesarea: "Madam, pray you.
Direct not thyself unto that subject,
'Tis of the essence for me to demand
For thee, to be sounded in wind and limb.
These are thy belongings; valued as ere,
(***He returns the handbag to Solania***)
And matter thee by keeping it awhile
Under my guardian."

Solania: "Ah! Don't utter that,
Thou mayst have it as thou list,
Ad infinitum I d'liver,
My princely greatest worshipper,

Unto thy strongest aid for bringing me
Here ~ quick."
(***She grasps Caesarea's hands strongly and admirably***)
"In this vainlier life of mine,
I've been imprison'd i' lornly state,
And all tides restrained by gloom.
My mirth of old hath been robbed,
Pitilessly speechless: tho' tiddly,
Running out from jocundity,
And befriended by nobody.
Thou my fresh and mild familiar;
Treating thee fast a young brother,
Shalt e'er fulfill my empti'dheart."

Caesarea: <(0) "Though a latency,[(M20)] sure I will sister.
(***He venerates and half jokingly with the word 'sister'. A doubt at first blush—Solania***)
"Matter thee 'gain twice, but thus far,
This is my prime time to flower,
Having and adoring a sister."

Solania: "Oho! There! Unto my surprise.
Art thou th' solely child of thine old lady?"

Caesarea: "Yea, sister. Ahome I've but a mater,
Whom acts everything a whole complete fam'ly—
Old man, a sister, and brother.
She is but the solely figure,
Whom hath caus'd to my delightness,
Thoughtful since time immemorial." [11] [M21]

Solania: "Oho! What a betimes pleasure!
Sonny, what's thy name, thereupon?"

Caesarea: "Caesarea. Mater oft-call'd me Aria.
(***Blurts him and continues:***)
As a hoi polloi o' an innermost village,
I oft-sang my self-compos'd melodies,
An alternative; brings me not on edge, [M22]
Flourished, but in depth of quietude,
And henceforth flitt'dly came my sobriquet.
And sister?"

Solania: "Shall Solania or Olan."
(***She unbuttons her handbag and gives Caesarea a wad of banknotes. Quoth she:***)
"I' naught betides thee awhile downtrodden world afar,
'Head discredit nay; oft-fully i' credib'lity, [M23]
My residence thy musical parlour, there'fter."

Caesarea: "Sister, thy gift a surpassing wonder,
For my minor, tiniest and banal aid.
This is not a wisely equality."
(***Twice, he has blurted tensely***)

Solania: "Sonny, there are extras awaiting thee.
Credit for thy viands in thy delight,
And benefit them thyself."

Caesarea: "I daresay that there
Aren't respecting abundant hours
To constitute for the purpose,
Forasmuch I've to make myself
For home betimes as demanded.
My uncouthly establishment, <12) (M24)
Refusing thine invitation,
Howsoe'er, thou'rt but to forgive.
Whatsoe'er foreshadows future,
I've conditioned my promise
To visit thee ayely anon."

Solania: "Thou mayst leave for th' destination,
Mere but, forget me do not behind,
I'm joy'd in forasmuch as o' thee ~ sonny,
Prithee! Unto my life comest thou."

Caesarea:

"Sure I Will, My Dear Sister" (S.iv)

Sung Verses (Song) (1st Refrain)

(*Verses in 7 syllables*)

Sure I will, my dear sister,
Thy words, th' tints in my journal,
Many a time I shall r'member,

Sure I will, my dear sister,
Feel heartsick thou wilt never,
I'm blithe unto thine Elysium,
Joyous will return—confirmed

Solania: "Thou shalt be, 'tis my glory." [*spoken*]

<u>Verses 1 & 2</u>

I' e'ery hue, glimmer'd th' em'rald,
Proud the wearer i' their vitals,
Thy descendants are th' vict'ry:
Spellbinding to th' eyes; sorely,
Aug'ring a forte; wax lum'nary

Jack-i'-th-box, a jocundly toy,
E'en a latter-day child or boy;
Phantastic'lly a bumper o' joy,
Be oft-pleas'd, ne'er gets wrothly,
May th' forenoon appears warmly;
Thee me a trifle actively

Solanla: "I'm impress'd with th' finely tune;
An elixir for my pain." [***spoken***]

<u>Refrain</u> (2nd & Closing)

Sure I will, my dear sister,
This gift for me, aplenty,
A phantasy below, rather;
Beseem in heaven, its worthy

Solanla: "'Tis but for this b'times special." [***spoken***]

Caesarea: "O! Very much I thank thee." [***spoken***]

Sure I will, my dear sister,
Thy history, I'm keen to hear,
For me an exclusive oldlore,
A great remembrance, evermore

Solanla: Possibly I may describe, [***sung***]
Promise thee when th' time is ripe,
If and will anon thou'rt here
Curv'd to revivify me.

Caesarea: I am lief to utter, yea! [***sung***]
"I'm bidding my impermanent adieu." [***spoken***]

Solanla: "May equanimity smiles upon thine
Homeward journey. And shall anon we see
Ourselves, again."
(***She smiles but inside, she is fast to weep***)

EXEUNT

Scene IV (The Hospital's Car Park & Kuala Lumpur City)

(***Poem is for Choir (=Narrator) or Caesarea's Mime Action. 8 syllables***)

Hot the sun, hot the lineament,
The infirmary boundary;
Raid'd hence by patient's variety,
Looking back; Olan's ir'descent,
Though his stomach burbles hungry

Widening his steps on one track,
Taking nay part'cular aspect,
Into his vast botheration,
Whereas in sole admiration

Walking while wiping sweatless head,
A progress is restless to treat,
Doing whatsoever is wise,
E'en to whatsoever the price

At the homely orange bus stop,
Ending his progression to clop,
On the long brick bench—verge's edge,
Sit him—shiv'ring like at old age;
Laud'tory: 'Th' moneys to engage.' [***whisper***]

Monologue

Caesarea: "Thee, starlit crypt in my sable feeling,
Thine arrival a hope of old of mine.
(***He counts the amount***)
"Wow! A glory pouring into my eyes,
But a misrule is here crossing my sense,
Altogether, seven thousand ringgits
Measured i' notes of one hundred ringgits;
I' a clodhopper calling major too great,
Whereupon unto me-financial,
Severally be beneficial,
Closing the fine's bill ~ an essential.
And my dear sister: one smile one moment,
I am grateful of thee for letting me
In this seventh heaven."

(***High on the firmament —an eagle has crowed between Caesarea's enjoyment***)

(***Poem below is for Choir (=Narrator) or Caesarea's Mime Action. Ordinary 10 syllables***)

Taking a min'bus, <15) (M27)
Which honourable routes he could e'er trust,
Apeak hours to th' city—non-trippery, (M28)
Ascending and descending i' brevity

Blithe his active spirit; nay raw deal,
But marred his visage by purblind thrill,
Die properly he would not laugh also won't,
But a fidgetily humor he hath shown

A hive of acts, unliquid; the Chow Kit,
Reknown ground the bounds of busy market,
His strong appetite is hence at its thrust,
Urging for Fried Chicken o' Ayamas

Hot-bloodedly enjoying it there will,
Just then, takeaway repast too a deal,
Breakfast hath been jocundly fulfill'd,
But whereto the police station—an ill!

Caesarea Exits

Scene V (Dangwangi Police Station & Puduraya Bus Station)

(*Poem below is for Choir (=Narrator) or Caesarea's Mime Action. Ordinary 10 syllables*)

Albeit sorely down: platitude's bound,
        But yet strides into th' Dangwangi's compound,
Respect's shown clearly in numbers of act,
        As well trying insomuch far from slack

5). **Dialogue**

Caesarea: "Morn well, Ma'am. Getting use to prime lesson,
While dessicating detrimental o' attitude
On driving throughout this coming future,
I would like to clear this bill."

Police Clerk: "A ven'rable start.
For what offence art thou being blamed?"

Caesarea: "I' grip!<16) (M29)
Stringilier to save someone's dread life,
I've insistingly driven licenseless,
But congratulating a try; least pick'd, (M30)
The patient hath passed the treatment quick."

Police Clerk: "Would The Creator bestow thee with luck."

Caesarea: "Thanks madam.
I am namby-pamby listing all these,
Here—few packed repast bought at ease,
Within my peaceable big heart to share
With thee and thy familiars."

Policeman: "What a whopper
I' this forenoon? Are these gifts to be impress'd;
Or contrawise to suggest ~ a treachery in th' zest?"

Caesarea: "In my argent hope shall 't not an offence,
I cherish, observe and heed nay pardon,
For my numbered, unwise but unselfish actions,
This my little share, small fortune I have,
A delight of being grateful—to pave."

Policeman & Police Clerk: "An acceptable av'nue to our vote of thanks,
Our response in view, just then not long a length."

(*Poem below is for Choir (=Narrator) or Caesarea's Mime Action. Ordinary 10 syllables*)

Hereafter the P.S. hath forsaken,
        But ne'er, the Puduraya Bus Station,
Scurrying for a ticket—but least cultured,
        While here and there judiciously alert

His additional pleasure; naught kernel,
        Journeying with bus of Trasnasional,
Setting forth homeward; surroundings an art,
        In man-made cold air his mirth in strong guard

ACT II

Scene I(A) (Merlimau, Malacca)

In the verdancy of a plantation but a garden, stuck a cottage of semi-Malayan ancient and semi-latterday Malay. Encompassing it, the nativity of pure equatorial fruits are betwixt their ripeness—jack fruits, rambutans, durians, and mangoesteens. On the grassy verge, Caesarea has just left the town bus; facing his dwelling, visage wax'd pleasingly. Losing sight of the previous events, temporarily. Emerging from the wide-open door—his mother.

1 A). Dialogue

Caesarea: "*Mere, je suis rentré! I have return'd home.* **(F.I)**
Une surprise d'après midi. Glory's foam'd." <18) (M32)

Ljiljana: "Aria, my concord bee. Real thou hath come?
Sweeping dust o' yest'rday ~ displeasure, anger,
A doubt a question. Wherefore tardy a day?"

Caesarea: "Mama. A day, when hath been stretch'd apart,
'Tis subjoin'd unto a little more story,
Naught err'd with my part, done but a bounty. (M33)
Sigh me for period's shrunk to expatiate, (M33)
If perchance at eventide I'd hav' made.
Mama pardon me, pray me once thou wilt,
For conundrums I had at sight: full tilt."

Ljiljana: "Do thy thing, but keep up the well-being,
Nay whiff of evil, luck's down to settle,
Here like lying o' satiety; heaven fine,
When I've thine amusing visage to dine,
Save aside, son. Run for the viands' bowl,
There, all inside, ere they're levell'd cold." (M34)

Caesarea: "*Mere, mere! Une surprise d'après midi.*
Un on-dit pas, vraiment. If thou art not moody." (F.II)

Ljiljana: "Dear, O! Dear good. And what are the such as
For particularly sure, here below?"

(***The suavely matron has replied rather wondering. She is an architect's pensioner with a score of psychological expertise. But likeably to live the way womanhood of a country at her wish***)

Caesarea: "*Celui-ci!* Hold something of disbelief." (F.III)
(***He gives Ljiljana the remaining banknotes***)

Ljiljana: "Circular dude's eyes! Whence thou'th obtain'd this?
(***Surprisingly she queries but apacely put another:***)
"Is this relate thy 'little more story'?"

Caesarea: "Yea, mama. From hand to mouth ~ paean paean!
And yet 'tis worth a small beneficiary,
Whereas numbers more 'yond in the waiting,
Or else hard upon."

Ljiljana: "Well! A fortune for thyself.
Thou keepest them.
(***She returns the money to her son and adds,***)
"Better wash thyself, now.
Think do's and don'ts. 'Bove, the revolution
Of the rack is sketching apacely; more,
A sign of rain."

Caesarea: "*D'accord! Je il ferai maintenant.*" (F.Iv)
(*He smiles warmly while keeping the money inside his bag*)

Ljiljana: "And therefore, actuate thy feet apacely."

(*The interior of the cottage is wide and spacious; roomless its feature. Bunk beds are placed at the corner. A mengkuang mattress is stretch'd over the small hall for general purposes. Caesarea's violin, guitar and oboe are left untouch'd for few days under the bed.*

Leaving his valuables on the mattress, he has thereupon changed his dress to merely a green shorts. Reaching for his towel on the hanger, he takes it and busily runs out to the outdoor bathroom. At the sight of his mother, Ljiljana, she is lauding the tenderly yet windy representation of the surroundings)

Ljiljana:

"Here I'm but on the Cloud" <19a) (S.v)

Sung Verses (Song) (*10 syllables*)
In my wise standpoint; beneath this tree joints,
A joyous occasion, this e'en to turn

All covetous sweet fruits are here again,
        Variedly instant taste to be enjoy'd,
Awhile the soothingly wind to attain,
        Ethereally hath put me oft-buoyed

E'ermore I'll bear i' my supplication,
Change in naught else this harmony of Orient

I've long in schooling; and hath well-vers'd,
        Critical junctures along I've shunn'd,
Whereon a degree a reward; ravish'd thus, (M37) <20)
        Forsoothly I've ascend'd—perfect a fun

Beneficiary of knowledge is hence
        Unto my fixed stand and well-grounded,
A gratitude much crutch for an experience,
        Unto my garland'd stand and well-founded

E'ermore I'll bear i' my supplication,
Change into naught else this serenely land

Pre-Refrain

I'm frettedly by this temporal life,
        Myriads o' muzz' blunder galant intruding, (M38)
Fly high be in-depth i' piety; sober dive,
        Awhile sacred practices are more to strive;
Further I invoke, all i' th' spur's ending

Refrain

Here I'm but on a cloud, on a cloud...
        Utter'd; lief I may for thine arrival—
Thee rainfall; th' actor of nature's wealth,
        I make a merit of this fruit season,
Another page of my pleasure; for certain

Here I'm but on a cloud, on a cloud...
        My son hath return'd; in hue o' fine fettle,
And's now enthrall'd by his little fortune

Caesarea: "Eureka! Mama, 'tis more than 'little'!" [*spoken*]
Ljiljana: "To thine heart's content, a laugh to extend." [*spoken*]

▬ ▬ ▬

(***Caesarea has his drench'd build sered by the towel. The windstorm that keeps rushing itself into the bathroom, has made the interior draughty. The boldness of daylight has dipp'd into the temporary shades of bleakly scenario. Startl'd he is in the cold, but ever meets for his jaded spirit. Barely to his credible spectacular, the surroundings are mere logically in presumption a lacklustre; but, has him been a sorely laggard in his reverie. A skirl of shout from Ljiljana has been thrice repeated ere it could capture his being lost to phantasy***)

Scene I(B) (Same Place)

1 B). **Dialogue**

Caesarea: "*Mere, qu'est-ce que c'est?* I forget." **(F.v)**
(***He responds a trifle withdrawn***)

Ljiljana: "Forget?! A smiling moon shouldst thou meet."
(***She blurts; wax'd in temper***)

Caesarea: "Those comically soothsayers've sold me
The smiling moon as a comestible.
(***He has jerked to realise; his old lady is in her angst ~ beyond compare***)
"Mama, many sorry. 'Tis all a skit-stir, <21) (M39)
Play'd by a rejected clown of old-timer."

Ljiljana: "Blockhead! On what spell art thou being charm'd?
Methought thou art betroth a maiden of fay;
Lapdog a loser by grace build a balm (M40)
Whereof the kisser lush a diamond spray." (M40)

Caesarea: "Beseem'd a javelin, th' wonder of nature,
Imbeds my heart; graceful I would gather:
But imaginarily pen'trative,
Hath sunk me into the deep o' reverie. (M41)
Alert'd! Pitch-dark while, arouse i' phantasy—
No way! No way but! I' a coffee barrel,
And err forsooth, for aught I know I hate
A toil 'yond lousy." (M42)
(***Thunder and rain begin***)

Ljiljana: "Whatsoever thy verse, comment I won't,
Hath belittl'd itself i' this thundercloud.
Standing there once more, like a day watchman;
Pretend'd sanctimonious, shall scent danger,
By and by meguess, thou facest the sod. (M43)
Think nay twice, apacely begone inside."
(***She urges solemnly***)

Caesarea: "Reasonably th' advice to acquiesce in."

(***He concludes alone. Simmer'd down, he runs into his house. Raindrops, like haricot beans, fall on his build apacely; a beat nonmusically in creation. Inside, he has spent his sorely unconsiderable time simpering at his mother. Clad in a newly raiment—Hawaiian knee-length bags*** (M44) ***and Marlboro Classic printed t-shirt; he smells the repast from within few feet away. Thereupon, he enjoys the viands***)

The Appetizing Viands (22) (S.vi)

(***Sung Verses for Choir = Narrator***)

Stood three dish's with rissoto; full o' colour,
　　Tasted to kill the surpassing hunger,
Big set ~ a sit-down luncheon for five men,
　　But to feed mere a mouth; diet, irrel'vant (M45)

The very first bowl; a mix-fri'd seafood,
　　And to detail; fishballs, cockles and prawns,
A crisp ambrosia, suits th' insipid mood,
　　Turn'd gaiety but caus's oft-def'cat'd adawn

The second bowl; a cuttlefish sambal,
        Dried cuttlefish i' a tangy hot gravy,
An occult to delated eyes small skull;
        Suit for in the appetite full of lull,
Thirsty pace but a delight i' 'ts entirety[(23)][(M46)]

The final the third bowl; a gravy pumpkin,
        Slic'd pumpkins i' sweet juicy coc'nut milk,
A delicate savour, village's special's seen,
        Watering the throat; a wiser choice to seek

Closing

A word from a gastronome, ere his silence;
Ere completing his appetizing viands.

▬ ▬ ▬

(*Trippingly Caesarea tells of the deja vu to his mother after the repast. Sombreness with nonsensical rhythm of the downpour on the cottage's roof-top of corrugated zink, has partly engulf'd his sounds of speech. Try upon try, he has endeavour'd a louder tone; and beyond the completion of his story at sundown— the rain has stopp'd. Delectably he has made a share-out of the sum; fifty-fifty with Ljiljana. And the old lady is stark won- derment in the spell*)

Scene I(C) (Same Place)

1 C). **Dialogue**

Ljiljana: "An event, shot through of spectacular.
Pity her e'er, a lame dog her quiver, <24) (M47)
'T befell her while lone i' a desp'rately need,
For thee 'tis such a meritoriously deed."

Caesarea: "I am specific that she's comradeless
Of her man and haply ere a viscountess;
But thus far sparsely, I see a lone heiress."

Ljiljana: "Stripling, my dear! Insulate such comment,
'Tis purblind heed to account her suchlike.
Howsoe'er to any degree of sort,
Our politics thus offer'd top status
Famous five: Dato', Tan Sri, Tun or Prince,
Including King Queen of course.
(***She breathes the cold air and elongates:***)
"I suppose,
Shall be betwixt morrow or two days 'yond,
With carriage we travel—abus at town,
To the infirmary; heartfelt tend her.
Uncertainly, she's unfair a plaything
Of her desp'rate inequitable world,
For this grandly value she hath present'd,

To earn our crutch and loving kindness—well;
Instinctivable, grace we should repay. <25) (M48)
Aria, far speak, for my felicity;
I'm proud, a younger brother she hath treat'd thee,
For thou livest in bourn o' nay sibling e'er, (M49)
Shouldst thou treat her anon a wonder."

Caesarea: "True mama. Rejoic'dly I'm in this still.
Imbed in my pate, thine advice, I will."

(***Amoonlit night, accompanies his humor in a jocundly light; haspersuad'd his intention, to play the violin. Avariation of self-compos'd serenade, duet with his mother on oboe, set at his will; have the night sparkl'd with thrill.***

EXEUNT

Two days later, as intend'dly by his old lady, they have betaken themselves unto the infirmary and visits Solania. The matron, with her deep-root'd feeling to commiserate, has put a strong disposition on Solania)

Scene II (A) (Interior of the University Hospital)

(First Shot on Scene A) / [6:30AM] (***On the narrow windowsill, the eagle with its eyes blinking (r.I.iv.par.18) has spaced a time admiring Solania. She is still sleeping. The bald eagle, crows deeply while pointing its vision at one of the passersby outside the corridor***)

[CUT/]

(2nd Shoton SceneB) / [7:15AM](*Adoctorandtwonurses enterthe room. Thebleak morn, within the vapid environment there, has influenc'd Solania into a consecutive abandon to grieve as she arises from bed. The doctor and the staff nurse try to converse with Solania, soothingly, while examining her*)

[CUT/]

(3rd Shot on Scene C) / [7:30AM] (*Caesarea and Ljiljana arrive with a plastic bag of breakfast and a kilogram of bananas. The bald eagle, howsoever, has taken its wing thereafter espying the two visitors while on their advancement into the ward/room*)

2A). **Dialogue**

Caesarea: "Good morrow, sister."

Solania: (*Utmostly delighted*) "O! My dear Aria."

Caesarea: "A way of prestige hard upon i' distance,
Prospering thy spirit not with silence;
Eat drink thy morn with tastes of elation,
Elude thereof wilt thou from annoyance."
[> To the Doctor:] "With sir physician—"

Doctor: "I'm pleased to meet thee."

Caesarea: [> To the Doctor:] "The careerist with his impress'd duty,
Giving cardinal treatment intensely,
But secure his patient's salubrity.
[> Back to Solania:] "Sister, sister my merry—"

Solania: "Close to me."

Caesarea: "Priding my immense hist'ry meeting thee."

Solania: "Aye!

Comest thou closer, let's be together.
Thine emergence, a marshmallow, hath freed me
From being captiv'd by ill'cit displeasure,
Inanimate space would that I could limn,
When ignoble methought thou'rt reluctant,
As e'er promis'd to return: O! Cold burnt,
For thy visage fills my heart that's sanguine."
(***She holds Caesarea's hands tightly and has smiled in contentment***)

Doctor: "Thy gravitas sister—grave dry lettuce.
In the greylier first place has restor'd not
By the vitamins of medicament,
Reposing in repudiation of healing,
When by stethoscope tested regular,
Morosely she is getting off-colour
Haply vanish thee her morbidity."

Caesarea: "Alas!
What a hit hearing; putting me aghast!
[> To Solania:] "Sister, unstare at impassivity,
I' I'm e'er to breathe, keep I'll my promise,
Or a blaze's spell o' curse thou shouldst put on my stat'd wish."
(*All the people in the room laugh*)

Staff Nurse:[> To Caesarea:] "What a breathtaking brother in my vaunt."
(***Staff Nurse sings Cavatina below***)(***7&10 syllables***)

"Vapidly though the weather,
        Demurely figures on spur,
But as green as the spinney,
        Like the boon engaged here,
Welcoming grand long brother,
        Magnified hath sated older sister,
When varnish'd company's presum'd soothing,
        Ant'biotics for em'tional coping,
Escaping from fungoid fur. (M50) <26)"

Solania: "It is comforting." [*spoken*]

Malay Nurse: (*Malay Nurse sings Cavatina below*)(*10 syllables*)

A magnesia is to cure a belly,
        Starving from oxygen, airs vexation,
Thereafter barbiturate is given,
        The patient is then again buoy'd and muzzy.
For us here, Doctor Karen Berkley quoth:
        'A lady's intense vulnerability,
Percepting fully unto the pain's node,
        In long distance of time; as well meetly
Lifting them to a Romano." (M51)

Doctor: "A wise prescription.
(*The people laugh again. Continues him,*)
"Here I discontinue my attendance,

Return might when the howlet's arriving,
Unto younger brother I would prescribe
Since a banana here precious a source,
A well lefty conceit in enriching
Healthy ingredients.
And must avoid most red-hot recipes,
More th' abstentation,
Widely on icebox items and liquor."

Ljiljana: "In our consideration."

The Doctor and the two Nurses exit

Caesarea: "Thanks to their counsel more and overly."

Solania: "They are valuable espousers of therapy."

Caesarea: "Sister Olan. This is my mere mater,
I bring here for thee; for the verity."

Ljiljana: "Lass, my standpoint. Let bygone be bygone;
And woeful misadventure let afar,
Take thy descendant a vanity of honour."

Solania: "Auntie, modest, I shall restore thy words.
Forasmuch of thee, myself like Aria
Hav' firm treated as a truelove mother.
Pray auntie! Invoke to the mirth of me;
Therefore kills th' cipher's taste (M52), thus far a nature." (27)
(*Solania has gripp'd Ljiljana's hands firmly with great emphasis*)

Ljiljana: “God’s bounty, bless’d you will to the feature.
Worst’d by intraceable foes of labour
Won’t e’ermore immure thee to dreariness,
But me, an old stager of this concern
Hav’ pain’d sol’taries; like native’th burthen’d,
Therefore be unflinching like me.”

Solania: “Such an advice
Won my admiration. Tho’ evil burns,
I try searching lost might. With ye I feel stronger;
Germane cheer.”

Ljiljana: “Lass, a pleasing repast o’ morn for thee.
A despair is an ill-omen; a ***cul-de-sac,***
Fair ‘twill cease by thy strong orison,
Fiddling about solemnly remembrance
May relive the lacerat’d heart of old,
Cowing bold like a troll beyond increment,
‘Twill put numbers o’ weight to thy shrunkenly
Young spirit.”

Solania: “I ditto. But... auntie,
If there is a wise day, comfortable for me;
Undistracted, thou shalt have an allotment
Of my story.”

(***She begins tasting the betimes repast of breakfast satiatedly. The matron pets Solania's lock of her pate ~ a tenderly care of a mother***)

Ljiljana: "Lass, shunning the tears apart tenders pain
The children whom we've deliver'd—a hardship,
Regardless their formation; queer mien seed,
Byword, our everlasting jocundity,
Tho' live as th' asset in vague verity."

Solania: "Hm!
A quantum passage.
(***Answers her soft awhile finishing the remaining breakfast. Jocundly thereafter,***)
"Auntie after all,
Doeth thou pray'd live with me?"

Ljiljana: "Within my discretion
As thou prefer'st."

Solania: "Oho! I'm lief taking."

(***They have convers'd till noon. Blabbing about social concern. The gap jumps to 2:30PM as shown by the wall clock. Solania thenceforth gives her dwelling's keys to Caesarea***)

Solania: "I may be releas'd i' th' next two fortnights.
Aria, pray watch th' house and those eggs for me.
(***She puts in determination. And to Ljiljana:***)
"I'm to blabber with thee again."

Caesarea: "Sister,
Sister, tiger is ever merciless,
But once a companion, whatsoe'er th' fay tale,
Hence let us forget our languor that burst,
When vapidness be paid by delightness,
Right 'twill change from wyvern to heaven's place,
Sister sister, thy benignly phizog,
A virtue to my being a joker i' th' future,
Sister sister, pray thee nay harm; my feature."

(*Solania laughs pleasurably*)

Ljiljana: He is untemperately with his jest,
Shall put thee laughing till watered eyes."

Caesarea: (*Adds with query of botheration*)
"Sister.
Matchy this key, cushy to use. Yet many buts,
Which house doeth it belong to?"

Solania: "Aria!
Doth thou not grabb'd by mem'ry?"
(*She cross-questions playfully*)

Caesarea: "Pardon me thou wilt,
That particular day, mere thee I'd cared."

Solania: (*Chortles and describes*)
Knowst thou one glimpse the yellow-painted house,
Add'd two solar panels on its tiled roof;
Cobblestone, its driveway and ere the gate
Liv'd a tamarind grove?"

Caesarea: "I' error not spelt
Is it th' one close to Arab Ashraf's resident?
(***He construes***)

Solanla: "Yea, sonny. Thou knowst it rightly."
(***Solania smiles as she looks at Caesarea. His lineament is full of grin***
[On the camera screen]

EXEUNT

[The screen is again faded to the hospital's car park. Then the camera zooms in on] ***Caesarea as he drives the Toyota Estima towards the main road***)

Scene II (B) (The Estima Interior)

2B). **Dialogue**

Caesarea: (***Manoeuvring the vehicle a trifle tremulously***)
"Cold breeze without, hot meat in. Singeing."

Ljiljana: "I view a bone man, not sore with his shudder, <29) (M54)
But I do not apprehend thee."

Caesarea: "Jumping,
Jumping in discomfort as th' police saith;
For me bilious unbreed, a dustbin dread,
But unto my sorely concern—blaming
Next bills of fine are i' my anxious sparring."

Ljiljana: "A trumpery suits a dweller o' a dustbin,
An offence is oft-repeated with keen,
When blindfold, merely the fine thou art think;
How is thy safety a roaduser in a blink?"

(***Caesarea has but grinn'd lily-livered***)

EXEUNT

Scene III (Tun Dr Ismail Garden, Damansara)

[A detail view in short succession about the house] (***A three stories bungalow; an impression of state-of-the-art architecture has liv'd desolately in its boundary.*** [Camera moves] ***Along the cobblestone driveway, the lamps on the decorative lampposts are left brightly shone. A collection of impressive Greek statuaries; in the form of three wenches, different style posted, have been a mystically decoration in the middle of a fish pond hard by the garage***)

[CUT/]

[A scarcely view of] (***a swimming pool with its stilly water, of pellucid light blue; of which is situated at the backyard of the house***)

[CUT/]

(***Ljiljana is interestedly watching a bird cage as she closes the car door***)

[CUT/]

[A close view of] (***the cage; dimension'd thrice the size of a crate has born merely two parti-colour'd parrots***)

[CUT/]

(***Caesarea is keeping his eyes peel'd at the oft-seen eagle***)

[CUT/]

[A quick close shot of] (***the eagle is parching upon a nearby palm tree which is swaying unto the wind***) [Outside the camera's focus] ***a sound of enthusiasm from the parrots***)

3). **Dialogue**

Parrots: "Halo! ***Monsieur***. Nobody is home now;
A lacklustre place's insipid to endow."

(*Caesarea and Ljiljana go jubilant*)

Caesarea: (*chortles as he responds*)
"Thy master is not here tending for thee;
Hardly utter'd, a patient o' labour pains,
And hath vilely laid i' th' infirmary.
We are here cock-a-hoop about befriend
Thee the dollies as a newly keeper,
Therefore pray, treat us nay an outsider."

(*The parrots in reply, make a wolf whistle with an animated style*)

[The scene is now cut to] (***Inside the house. The commodious interior is compact'd with musical instruments. Six guitars, ranging from classical, jazz, flamenco, and pop, alongside with a mandolin are arrang'd on their stands in circle***)

[CUT/]

[A close shot of] (***A Wagner grand piano and two synthesizers on stand with their assembled multi-racks are converg'd at the hall. Two fine violins and a violoncello are plac'd readily to be play'd; beside, few mountable combos and amplifiers. On a teakwood bookshelf, its space has been fulfilled with musical references)***

[CUT/]

[A quick view of Caesarea's reaction] (***He seems delightfully rivet'd but shortly hence has behav'd emotionless unto the glamour.*** [The camera is now tracking as] ***He apacely brings the box of the fiv' eggs upstairs of which is on the second floor***)

[CUT/]

(***Ljiljana is watching him from the hall***)

[CUT/]

[Tracking Caesarea as] (***He enters one of the six rooms view'd, and leaves right after he has placed the eggs on a large king-size bed. As he walks downstairs, he takes a brief study at the objects along the carpeted corridor***)

[CUT/]

[A medium angle shot] (***Olden and latter-day artifacts are in a surpassingly display. On the walnut panel'd wall, a collection of several species of mummified eagles, are beseem'd a semblance of grisly myth. Overly bemused, Caesarea has turned.*** [Low angle shot of his legs as] ***he stops before the stairs.***)

[CUT/]

[A close view of] (***His lineament ~ full of adoration by another unusual observation***)

[CUT/]

[A close shot of] (***A table with leopard heatis, reminiscent of the Pharoah's grandeur; another bald eagle which is sculptured in silver, is likely to guard a scroll of poem of which is hung betwixt the cranny of its beak***)

A coxcomb forsooth verbally welly wott'd,
    But a benign stripling o' but proudless deed,
A treasure to hope and laud; fervent hot,
    Though of bestial ancestry; least heed

[CUT/]

[A scene downstairs. Camera is now tracking as] (***Caesarea lingeringly brings over a tray of Sunkist orange's cold drink, from the kitchen towards the hall. Presumably as viewed, has shown that Caesarea is as if accustom'd with the house***)

3A). **Dialogue**

Caesarea: "Albeit this outré pecuniary gain, <30) (M55)
In tie-up, these're all peculiar for me,

Tho' gaily to graze all the wonderment,
Like long chord able to use them freely
Farthest love, I'm clove to sister Olan,
Whereby these diversely treasures, eyed golden;
For the poor a sorely admiration,
Otherwise to th' satanically lure,
A despicable heart; a surpassing tenure.
Undissolute's us, tendentious for naught,
But sanguinely still a bliss to adore.
Mama, this fine drink wets better thy throat,
Initiating unto this wonder, more."

Ljiljana: "Like phantasmal objects, I'm to observe;
All pure perfect. Within their distinction.
But Aria, there aren't our proper belongings.
Try seclude thyself from slipshod using,
Especial a concern whene'er the owner
Whereabouts is not apparent."

Caesarea: "***Mere, je connais.*** **(F.vi)**
I am ditto unto thy menu." <31) [M56]

Ljiljana: "Bear!
A quarter of my phrase; don't divorce need
Thou shouldst act wise if counted unvain,
Sketchily those o' mine, a landmark for thee,

Establishment divine; nay th' pestilence,
With that hung portrait, it determines me;
For inquiry meet, couldst thou behold 't?
Double concept. In my standpoint a stalwart;
E'er I'd guess he's her man of whom hath lost."

[A close up of Jannequin's portrait]

[CUT/]

[A low angle shot of] (***Caesarea's hands running on the piano keyboard. Awhile running his fingertips on the piano—rhythmically melodic, he sings his imperfect notion***)

Caesarea:

If Perchance <31a) (S.vii)

Sung Verses (Song) [***Mixed syllables***]

Interpreted—shall list as an epic,
    Ingressing into times of old; but mock,
Speaking my peace touching him; mine is weak,
    Visage there, but thus storied mere a log

A glimmer like a familiar the fowl,
    High on welkin one forsooth an eagle,
Like chip of the old block, a man; the soul,
    Keen sight; sensitivity a nonpareil

Refrain

If perchance
Would that mine nay a trumpery,
Lost not him; hitherto pristinely-hence,
But live a beast, unflinchingly

If perchance
To my hardcore humor; nay phantasy,
An occult 't beseems; a trueborn Occident~
Within glance,
(**Ljiljana**) [interpolates:] "Stick and stare, revere hence thence."
But an archaic subject; list'd bootlessly

▬ ▬ ▬

Ljiljana: "Whatsoe'er the bilge, I presume not vain
A jest for the liege. O'erly I'm involv'd,
Aria, wherein live the eagle, therefore?"

Caesarea: "Make not flesh creep, 'tis there whereto my trip."

Ljiljana: "Thus far seen, is he in the whereabouts?"

Caesarea: "Yea. Beyond hearsay, about and without
This house he hath oft-flown, rested and stay'd."

Ljiljana: "I' he showeth his visage e'en sordidly display'd,
But nay th' one scoundrel of brutality,
He is byword a gallant forsoothly."

EXEUNT

Scene IV (Solania's Bungalow, Driving Test Compound— Petaling Jaya, and University Hospital)

(***Poem is for Choir = Narrator or Caesarea's Mime Action***)

In th' luxuriously impressive dwelling,
E'ermore bewitching his pleasure o' living,
A feather on his cap; th' musical parlour,
Composing 'yond symph'ny is i' to gather

At one time chancing his locomotion,
Reck compuls'ry to own a driving license,
Tho' rat'd telling till letter'd; th' procedure,
But hate twice misdemeanour must endure

The branded fiv' eggs, his surpassing vaunt,
And hav' fastly foreshadowed time to hatch,
But fortnightly hav' instinctively gone,
Yet, changeless; less perchance a baffling batch

A forethought is unusual his conduct,
Forgathering a mate his will, but hard;
Sister Olan hath him bedd'd in her heart,
For the nonce but yet beat her breast apart,
And arose a living statue but a shard

Still, baker's dozen he and his mother,
Tracking th' akin road to th' infirmary,
Howsoe'er sis Olan's lurgy a hint—drear,
But his amusement—she's a bit rejoic'dly

A moon hath passed, she is fitly released,
But belittl'd e'er from rejuv'nation,
Sits—drawn on a wheel chair, hath sorely list'd;
Enviously unto the post'd limn'd gallant

A red-letter day of someone,
Worths a moiety to a loyal familiar,
In a morn of esprit; pathos none,
Sister Olan in her leaning posture;
Is at own will oping her nostalgia

[The camera is viewing the scene after breakfast in the decorative kitchen] (In due course, while keeping her forbearing countenance, Ljiljana finishes washing the dishes. [The camera is hence tracking at] Ljiljana gaililyjoins Caesarea and Solania at the living room. (r.II, iii. Par.18 above)

4). **Dialogue**

Solania: "Auntie, burthen thyself not with the clean.
Stifl'd my limb unlike thy bouncy son,
For heartsick, yet despis'd, led to mine ailing build."
(*She contrites while resting on the chesterfield*)

Ljiljana: "Lass, speakest thou not touching th' affliction,
Thou shouldst be jocundly i' gradation,
Upon thy recovery by and by.
Me mater whom hath list'd nought from her child,
Merely their e'erlasting contented smile,
So lass, use thine humor for ultimate
Relaxation. Profit if alleviate
Thy discomposure."

Solania: "Aye auntie... and, Aria?
[The scene is cut to give a close shot of] (***Caesarea whom is playing the violin, surprisedly jolts and stops***)

Caesarea: "Yea sister?"

Solania: "Aria, doeth thou list hearken (M57) <32)
The account of this fiv' eggs?"

Caesarea: "Sure, i' thou art
In foray to reveal." (***He responds pleasantly***)

Ljiljana: "Lass, art thou even
Rejuvenated limning such a story? (M58)

Solania: "Lest perchance this is my last will auntie,
To reminisce and revive the events,
I' I'm to be gathered to my fathers then,
O'erly I'm assuaged."

Ljiljana: “Lass, mention musn’t
Touching death. For I revolve thee i’ my orison
A breed of everlasting cheer.”

Solania: “Auntie!’

(***She embraces the old lady, bedew’d eyes with tears***)

[CUT/]

[A shot around] (***Solania tells of her remembrance from the outset. And she sings Cavatina*** **[(S.viii)]** ***for the Sonnet below***)

“A fat’d event, happen’d three years ago,
When as a lawyer; a work an imbroglio,(<33) [(M59)]
An odd woman out of the other staff,
For phasing fellowship in—unenough,
Weather’d by my fashion o’ stolidity,
For my being indulgence since new baby,
One for the book; many cases I’ve won,
And one occassion; ‘mazedly I was thrown,
‘Twas an onerously criminal’s case,
But a substantial ‘sset for ‘non promotion, [(M60)]
For i’defensible the crucial prospectus,
A f ’lony o’ attempt murder—the accusation,
Jannequin his name I was fond knowing,
Thence th’ short gaol our relation’s beginning.”

[The picture dissolves to ACT III, Scene I]

EXEUNT

ACT III

Scene I (Campbell Police Station)

The police station is amidst a hive of activity. Few hoggish juveniles with hands enchain'd by handcuffs of doubt'd trespass are waiting on the bench, laxly; awaiting to be bail'd off. Thought as a symptom of social disease.

Solania proceeds into the interviewing cell, accompanied by a stodgy policewoman with a rank of constable.<34)

1). **Dialogue**

Policewoman: "Many of the bucks over there are to stand by their goofy fashions.(M61) Rolling with the same fiendish sickness."

Solania: (***Assuming them a piddling detail she puts others***)
"Haven't you heard any tidings 'bout him?
Finite my spring for this gaug'd Jannequin."

Policewoman: "I'm gazing a surrender as mere spooky,
But he's gaudily for my perception, (M62)
Though geniality calling women,
Spare gawkiness not or covet'd by his finesse."

Solania: "Deducting my derisory d'pendence."
(***As Solania walks into the cell, the W.P.C. has then stood outside ~ a sentinel. Presumed a sequestered spot, she meets Jannequin***)

[CUT/]

[A close up of Jannequin] (***A profile, a nature of semi-Italian with a slender nose, deep watery eyes and rugged with long hair in ponytail; has sered by inglorious and vainly circumstance but howsoever remains sangfroid. His crinkly raiment with pureless sanitariness has proved the marr'd cheer of him.***

Burying her head in the sand, Solania forsooth is beseemed captivated by his emergence; and has drawn her queries with smile)

1). **Dialogue**

Solania: “Holding by this statement, thou’rt suppos’d traced
Phillip’ Jann’quin; sobriquet o’ ‘Piger’.”

Jannequin: “Yea Mistress.
(***He answers urbanely but has put another***)
“Touching my downtroddenly judg’d misdeed;
Is there much any likelihood indeed
To prove I’m not foredoom’d to guilt counsel?”

Solania: “My mould’s not to depreciate a client’s need,<35) (M63)
But forthrightly, worth naught I’m than angel,
Except obliging, Monsieur Jannequin;
As much value as ‘tis within the bound
Of my accomplish’d and letter’d standing.
My merely ardour’s to guard and beside
Thy granted verity as innocent.”

Jannequin: “My affordity’s in the position,
But millionaire’s none my equal measure,
And a prisoner I’m impounded by seizure.”

Solania: “But I simplify this a gratis work;
Valuing the gratuity middling perk,
Somehow I demand thy greatest tol’rance,

And moreo'er thy principal confidence.
Merely aplomb satisfies thy wishes,
By and by I'm willing to oblige thee."
(***Softly she has utter'd the very last sentence***)

Jannequin: "***Merci!*** <35a) [F.vii]
Madame. Merci!"

Solania: "***Ne vous en faites pas.***" (***Answers her in French***) [F.viii]

Jannequin: "Madam, apprehendest thou French?"

Solania: "Me, not that fluent.
But treat e'ery word wise a remembrance,
Slit misquotations, gloomy a foreigner."

Jannequin: "Bedew'd hath my sharp eyes for God's pardon,
This's thrice my leisure."

Solania: "***Monsieur, attendre!*** [F.ix]
But few o' thy sentenc's within permission.
'Thers, strictly English."

Jannequin: "I'm a doubting Thomas,
Mind thee, counsel."

Solania: "Funny, witty words utter less.
(***She inhales the stuffy air and mercurially continues,***)
"My Monsieur Jannequin, whence art thou come?
And rehearse how did it happen?"

Jannequin: (***narrates or sings the sestain below***)(***Mixed syllables***)

"***Je suis une autochtone de Lyon***, <36a) **(F.x)**
Beseems an inquiring place,
With purlieusly pristine space,
Sans maintenant; pas pertinence, **(F.xi)**
For as much a history,
For the nonce mere unworthy

Believing's understanding; wouldst thou not,
I'm a noble a century ere Jacobite,
A resplendent seigneur in his fine pride,
But my plodd'd nature hath willing to thwart,
Insipidity—a nature of a beast,
Suspending a wistful heart in the least

Taking my brain off th' irrel'vant topic,
By and by voyaging with a vigour,
At wind end I was a licens'd victualler,
Here an Occident merchant; I'm frolic,
To a r'velry o' stranger; nay the rationale,
But the play'd game is not worth a candle

When I astir the next improper morn,
Squalidly in blood and mud I was left,
In a red car with a pistol I'd slept,
Wayside in the ditch, a corse was laid prone,
Had holed chest and vesture turn'd into shreds,
I was i' o'er my pate; Drat! Smelt many rats

Though deuced dread; but had in for fastness,
Yet not touch'd a scintilla of the chance,
Th' police arrival; I was i' a nuisance,
I've limn'd the events but all bootless,
All time squatting with harrowing humor,
When I was indicted a murderer

An indignity; trammels of my life,
After six advocates refuse my case,
Indel'cately presum'd a defense of waste,
'S there a cast-iron al'bi, acquits me 'live?
An answer I'm sorely sorely beseech,
And thus begone this ~ a pretty kettle o' fish."

Solania: "Couldst thou recall thy strange partner there?
The dinner round? The moment ere th' event?"

Jannequin: "Yea. But, th' man with sobriquet Ravioli,
Is now under the police's int'gral hunt,
But vain thus far, three moons I'm already,
There's not a single sign of his whereabouts.
Madam pray, I'm loony i' withstood a moon more."

Solanla: "Monsieur Jannequin, in the entirety
I apprehend th' obnoxious situation,
But thou art ineluctable—methought,
Unto this mere provisional mischance.
Somehow a privilege o' delight'dprescient,
Most my assurance, but's delimited
To unknown, yet crit'cal circumstanc's 'non.
(She reads from a written statement)
"Already the cloud are thy fingerprints
On th' semi-automatic revolver—
Zero point three eight caliber Ruger; (= ***0.38***)
And full in'briat'd for o' alcohol influence.
(***She pauses with a short breath***)
"But contrawise to th' characteristic
O' expedient is ben'ficially number'd;
First, a heavy drunken man couldn't b' able
Handling a del'b'rate shot o' more than fiv' bullets,
At considerable time of an hour,
With the suggestive bullet's cases were unfound.
Secondly from the autopsy's report,
Th' semen o' which had been spott'd and ident'fied
In th' victim's vagina is not equat'd
With thy blood sample."

(***Another short breath while glancing at the W.P.C.***)
"Third, th' acknowledged fashion as a guiltless wight
I' th' morn where the arrest had taken place—
Is another advantage o' additive.
Howsoe'er, th' one whom hath maltreated thee,
Invalidat'd their profession'lism; [(37)] [(M66)]
Th' harsh-entreat'd but beneficial elk's meat, [(M67)]
Their precedence's to put thee i' custody.
Fourth, a new lease o' life for thee. Th' strange companion—
Ravioli Abdullah, whom a want'd figure,
Now's consider'd lost from the sight o' judgment.
Tho' advantages beseem in perspective,
But's not interdependently with the
Final unpronounc'd effect, thereupon."

Jannequin: "Perish the thought, Madam!, Perish the thought!
Consume I will the dust on thy raiment,
Servile 'bedience I put 'pon my shoulder,
To thy desire for exaltation."

Solania: "Thou'rt assuming me thus a dairymaid?
With th' verses—servile obedience and on?
Art thou strongly apprehend'd or merely
Dallying with these?"

(*Questions her sarcastically; seriously not, but towards an afternoon jest. Flying apart his hand, Jannequin has caught her crook of the arm. She allows it as it is*)

Jannequin: "Sit my brain; melt'd spirit—lay my humor:
Not at all with me the inglorious mien,
Tho' imbuedly accus'd a basely actor,
Once a convict, th' good, vainly to ascertain;
A specimen o' villainy in'luctable
T' augur. Honey'd verse but insincere not;
Tho' sketch'd disdain, but, by and by welly's certainty
Thou wouldst gather."

Solania: "My Monsieur Piger,
Translated thus as Mister Understand!
(*She squeezes his nose high-handedly; smilingly awhile arising to leave, she has reassur'd:*)
"Heart and spirit too believe thy utt'rance,
But enough here this trivially conscience,
Extends it further never to the court
Awhile jurispudence-literate to nod (38) (M68)
Though less than a jurist; effort a mount (M68)
This one trial, I shall accomplish, surmount.
Howsoever rest thine hope not upon
The willingly answer."

Jannequin: "Apprehend'dly
Throughout whim verily I am."
(***He discerns unnervedly***)

Solania: "Meet thee
At the court of justice."

(***Ends Solania soft. She leaves the cell with the W.P.C. But before she could advance her pace, he has stopp'd with few words***)

Jannequin: "My Madam, I revere
Th' way thou standst. Pray! Thou shouldst help me
Wherever possible, and the reward
Is thy treasure henceforth."
(***Solania glances back at him with a nod; and proceeds without the place in brevity***)

Policewoman: [> to Solania] "I expect your hearty measure from him."

Solania: (***smilingly***) "I suppose I shall be more than yours, Miss."

(***In Solania's rattl'd heart, has fill'd thereafter a scintilla of fondness towards Jannequin. And beseems in a fool's paradise. Outside, the weather is rather humid and pressurising***)

EXEUNT

Scene II (A) (The Criminal Section Court II, Jalan Raja, Kuala Lumpur)

(*Hazy aura does look'd like nothing on earth. The scene is now shifted to [pan] Jannequin, of whom is escorted by a policeman into the court's yard. His eyes, bulged forasmuch as of sleeplessness. His mouth is numbed and the visage—arrantly ashen. In ascension into the court's room, where his case will be heard, he has reckoned a vapid glance at Solania*)

[CUT/]

[The scene now focuses on] (***Solania with a complete aspiration to battle for the rightful claim of his being sinless howsoever, is aghast at his unkemptly aspect***)

2A). **Dialogue**

Solania: "Monsieur Jannequin, shows none if any
Contemptuous understanding 'pon thyself,
Th' court concerns much on well arbitration,
With mainstay[(M69)], get not unnerv'd apacely, <39)
Hav' a good aspiration o' something worths best."
(*She accosts in a short length away*)

Jannequin: (*In a vapidly smile, he replies,*) "Madam—"

Solania: (*But Solania has interjected apacely*)
"Call me Olan, my Monsieur Jannequin."

Jannequin: (*simultaneuously grins and elongates*)
"Olan, I'm ne'er volatile relying on thee,
Furthermore, I have my choices merely aslant
On thyself ~ readily."

(*Solania answers with a jovial smile*)

[CUT/]

(*The scene is now shifted into the court room. The condition has changed insipid and abstemiously solemn. Actually, it is the fourth day of the trial. Crowds of onlookers but absence of juries)*

2A). **Dialogue**

Judge: "Be seated. This court is now in session.
I felt draught last day. Not'fiable not now,
Misgiving I behold th' prosecutor,
The fourth day hence for the solicitor,
Elucidat'st hence thou with eloquence."

Prosecutor: "Your Honour, I shall examine my sweat."[<40)][(M70)]

Judge: "Ill-natured is legal mere for thyself,
Carry on the lady solicitor."

Solania: "Thanks Your Honour. I'm seriously intend'd.
(*She glances at Jannequin, whom is standing in the dock*)
"I ignite: my client, Phillip' Jannequin,
Accus'd blindly a felony o' murder,
The mid-night of twenty first of August,
Stonor Road K.L.'s regard'd not guilty,
Depending on sev'ral motives pil'd here."

Judge: "Thou'rt indistinguish'd being such laggard,[(M71)]
Declare thy several information,
I admit nay laughter forth."

Solanla: “Though ‘tis a damper
Of a value with less sprywitnesses, (M72) (41)
A stronghold on his side. Howsoever
This man would be sagely presumed a dupe
Of an insidious maltreatment.”

Prosecutor: “In what corner
Shall ‘t be presented?”

Solanla: “Verity on assumption.”

Judge: “Good. This is a heavyready criminal case.
Pray propound th’ angle.” (M73)

Solanla: “The victim herein
Witted as Yvon Laurel. Prominent
A career as a look’d for nightclub dancer,
Whom, betimes nine at night, had been plunder’d,
Fixed in the statement by the corse’s surgeon,
Pathologist the science is sufficient,
Or fitly consider’d term the first proof.
Whereby meantime th’ defendant, accord’d,
Was there, within the party whereabouts.
Herewith I would opine further as broad
As a pyschologist.”

Scene II (B) (In an Apartment at Pandan Indah Nuri Court)

(***Solania's Voice***)

'Miss Yvon ere,
May hav' a secret conflict with her partner—
Ravioli; a roommate or a lover,
In her premises—Nuri Court, Pandan.
This is stat'd by third witness—Helena,
Of whom'd prior exclud'd her identity
From the public."

2B). **Dialogue**

Yvon Laurel: "Ravioli, avaunt thee. AVAUNT!
Look... ne'er I shall this toilet shape,[<42)][(M74)]
Nay knock, nay touch that valued door.
Avaunt and avaunt desert forth."

Ravioli: (***Still knocking outside***) "O-oo!
Wherein desert should I begone?
Wherein glade should I arch'dly sleep?
Tell me love, if not on thy kindly bed."

Yvon Laurel: "I hate thee all my gaucherie,
Hate this villain hence turns a spell."

Ravioli: "Then spoil th' spell!
Disparage my buttress o' lewdness never,[(M75)]
I tell thee I've disagreed to be 'way,

This second kingdom; thee my smooth flower,
Think my charity, but thou art my imp;
When night princess thee is facilitat'd
From garbage courtesan o' Tiong Nam alley.
Spasmodic my content; rude 'bove randy,
I have from a ranked lady is marred! MARRED!
Yvon, cycle thine intellect. Which thou listest?
Enhance my stay, or outside thy snob's way?

Yvon Laurel: "Hark wilt thou? The last!"

Ravioli: "Not mine, it is thee.
Loathed chumming with chump ends chronicly,
Even choked off I never surrender.
Cycle thine intellect. Churlish a nighter,
The blacklier the first number; chuckle's fuss,
There I recrudesce one might fiv' lovers
At once."

Yvon Laurel: "Muddl'd be thy threat. I plead nay recourse,
Avaunt thee."

EXEUNT

Scene II (C) (Jalan Stonor, Kuala Lumpur)

(***Solania's Voice***)

'Yond infraction, he'd conspir'd with mates o' cur,
Estimat'd about fiv', and murder'd her;
Wherein the locale, the Jalan Stonor,
In the seventh late night stat'd thereafter.'

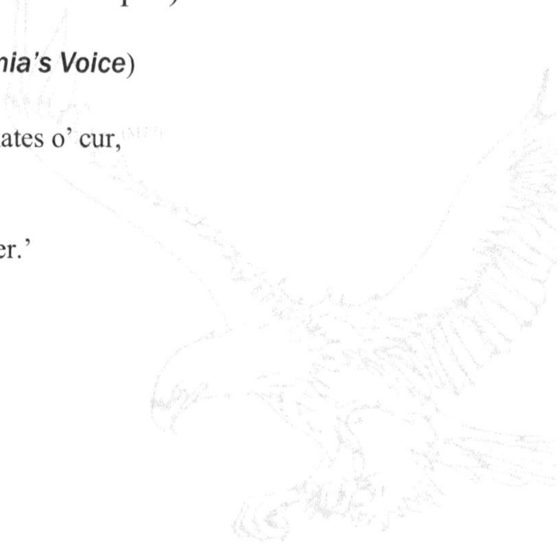

2C). **Dialogue**

(***Yvon's eyes are blinded by handkerchief with enchained hands***)

Yvon Laurel: "Who are ye in the dark? I couldn't see but's trapp'd,
Wherein dungeon I'm gaoled momentarily?"

Ravioli: "Cycle thine intellect. Churlish is at its apt
Darkest."

Yvon Laurel: "Damn thee! Damned till eternity!
O! Dear fear. I'm unmeritable for."

Ravioli: "Violence

Is centralis'd. I'd like thee to make a companion,
Shortliv'd but with feeling. Hark their laughter."
(***Unseen strangers laugh and laugh continuously***)

Yvon Laurel: "O! Dear horror. My world is receding."

Ravioli: "And.. and,
Shall deplete the frame of thee, smooth flower."

(*Solania's Voice*)
'She had thenceforth severely molested,
Engulfed by consternation so rapid,
Th' grevious bodily harm—drove her berserk.
Stimulated by her chaotic shriek;
Concomittantly ginger to ruin her,
Had slit in their brief murderous order,

And immediately fired six bullets,
Three on the nape, three rest about the chest,
Followingly, left the corse in the ditch.'

EXEUNT

Scene II (D) (Bukit Mas, Melawati — Klang Valley)

(***Solania's Voice***)

'Ravioli ere had befriend'd Jannequin,
Casual met at Semua House discotheque,
Confront'd a lewd outline—he was downright,
And hence abused Jannequin; per'lous plan,
Invit'd th' defendant to party ~ prime step,
Left him 'twixt eight and ten—for the murder.
'Bout ten tardily join'd the defendant,
Persuasion stirr'd with pretend'd revelry.'

2D). **Dialogue**

Ravioli: "'C'mon man. Once, to-night, be hearty heighten'd,
The V.S.O.P. is pure than Heineken,
Instantaneous then, impress to bustle,
In gleam glen and glee(M78). Thou shalt eye and thrill'd,(<44)
'Cmmon man. Wastage ne'er a bit. Drink them all."

Jannequin: "Sorry, I can't afford."

Ravioli: "Last and that's all."

Jannequin: (***Looking sleepily at Ravioli***)
"Fine for a mate's instigation."
(*He gulps the liquor till end*)

Ravioli: "Behold!
Instantaneously visit'd by th' duchess."
(***Enters a duchess***)

Jannequin: (***Stares blurrily at an ignorant beauty***)
"My pate is swaying so I'm not impressed.
Lord! Unto the glebe I'm flopping to rest."

(***Solania's Voice***)
'He was then menaced as Ravioli's prey.
Later the accus'd was stilly driven,
Th' aforemention'd place was final assay,
Left a sole figure for th' accusation,
Thereby had the devil and the others
Impeccably escap'd."

EXEUNT

Scene II (E) (The Criminal Section Court II, Jalan Raja, Kuala Lumpur)

2E). **Dialogue**

Judge: "A fine exposure,
Thus, any objection?"

Prosecutor: "Yea Your Honour.
Tho' lies a representation o' evidence;
Subjected a defence, but facsimile
Genuine second'ries[M80] as many observ'd.[46]
More solid proofs are deem'd necessary."

Judge: "The presumption of innocence as bound
In the Act Procedure's deem'd cons'quential
To fortify minor proof from the search.
Thus' relevant and accepted."

Solania: "Thanks Your Honour.
(*She hands a photostated document to the judge*)
"From this sign'd pathology's statements here,
Declared y'stermorn[M81] ~ I could proper protest.
'Tis passively trivial with th' solid proofs,
Tho' fingerprints on th' gun and urine test
Is him and to him the imposing importance.
'Cause[M81] primely, nay consider'd fingerprints
Found o' th' victim's build relates th' defendant.
Secondly, the seminal fluid tested
Differs from his blood sample."

Prosecutor: "Object Your Honour.
The murderer might have practised a sheath
Suggestively."

Judge: "Objection's accepted.
I' terminus th' second proof as considered,
Pray carry on with the third valuation."

Solania: "In the medical test; testified neat,
The accused's[(M82)] positive with drug's 'mount [(M82)]; <47)
Ecstasy pills o' psychedelic potence,
Which's held by Section Thirty Column Fiv'
Poison Act of Year Nineteen Fifty-Two,
And too was absolutely overdrunk.
Therefore, th' attempt of complete stranglehold,
Accused i' Section Three-Two-Six, Crim'nal Act,
Rationally a neg'tive del'b'ration.
For a dreamer's ephemera within episodes
Is a negated entity to pleasure;
None a strangler, neither a murderer,
Nor rapist."

Judge: "This's consider'd as premier,
Though the effect's still carried for understudy.
As time makes its full stop thus the dissolution,
This case shall be heard again, morrow nine.
The court is now adjourn."

EXEUNT

Scene III (Same Place)

[A quick shot of] (***Jannequin's aspect is in a blink of inglory***)

[CUT/]

(***Solania is focusing her attention at the prosecutor***)

[CUT/]

(***The prosecutor is now introducing a witness who tries to inculpate Jannequin***)

[CUT/]

[The camera zooms in on] (***Mister Brown walks into the court room. He is an Englishman; standing stodgy with a somberly visage. After taking under oath, he is questioned***)

3). **Dialogue**

Prosecutor: "Mister Brown, pray present th' detail'd account
About this man's action there on that night.
If manageable be concise but just."

Brown: (***watches Jannequin while describing***)

"By my count,
From eight thirty till nine at night aright,
He was initiat'd by th' party thru'[M83] my gauche eyes.[48]
As time elaps'd, improperly had his type,
Mixed trifling while on edge's significant,
With a peculiar laughter proceeded.
Suddenly, he was loss for an hour,

Upon return he looked pretty fatigue,
Solemnity o'erlapped with lame delight
Instilled my curosity. Thus shortly
Presumed his askance satiety."

Prosecutor: "Your Honour,
By his light description; sketchy referred,
We could apprehend that the defendant
Fixedly interrelat'd to the murder.
Here I'd accentuate the accuse's intent
Naught but gunning an insidious getter. <49) (M84)
Accessory to th' premeditat'd act.
He was again reused to th' downright fact."

Solania: "I object Your Honour."

Judge: "E'erybody's sweating. Yea, an inquiry."

Solania: "Mister Brown. Wast thou not being accompanied
By any lady during that stat'd night?
Pray answer ~ aye or nay."

Brown: "Yea."

Solania: "Fair statement."
How frequent thou hath lapsed observing
The defendant due personal matters?"

Prosecutor: "I object Your Honour!
(***Interpolates the prosecutor as he adds,***)
"This's consider'd
Irrelevant."

Judge: "Objection's overruled,
Pray extend thine answer Mr Brown."

Brown: "B'yond
My wiseable thought, less perchance."

Solania: "No more
Your Honour."

Mr Brown Exits
[CUT/]

[A shot on another witness] (***The twelfth witness. A bartender who has served the party; providing his statements beside Jannequin***)

Prosecutor: "Here comes the twelfth witness. Pray describe
Mister."

Bartender: "I'm a bartender at the Poppy Bar,
He was a likeable customer by general,
Though he'd behav'd spruce, expressly pleasant,
But was disconsolately lined to limp
By persuasion for wine by familiars,
Till he was trapped in heavy drink."

Solania: "What didst
Thou spectate more in th' situation?"

Bartender: "The man as witted
Ravioli'd plunged a capsule in the glass
O' Remy Martin, rapidly at th' counter
Ere presenting to that man."
(***He points at Jannequin***)

Solanla: "When's this taken place?"

Bartender: "After his absence o' about two hours since
Eight thirty that night."

Prosecutor: "Art thou a genuine
Spectator of the scenes?"

Bartender: "Truly I am."

Prosecutor: "Wherefore such act as a recognition?
Bartender: "I was dispirited to meet an oom." [pron. = ʊəm]
Whom was a victim o' a kind invitation,
And I'm intransigent to prove a clue,
E'en hav' gun blasted, my ghost is still fresh
To correct th' indispensable event."

Judge: "Though merit a jocosity for thee,
Th' twelfth witness, but I feel thy twinge twisted.

The Bartender Exits

(***The court room has changed to a brief laughter***) [The screen then fades] [Ashortviewof](***Thefollowingwitnesses—abusinessman, ahairdresser, and a journalist. First, the businessman*** [at a close shot], ***viewing Jannequin as a business associate)***

Businessman: "I admire him a reasonable trader,
But when questioning my tribute or praise,
I'm trilateral for this decision,
Grandly when touching o' conduct; I'm fussy,
But about him I'm in a thrice support."

Solania: "Hath not he ever admitt'd misleading resort?"

Businessman: "As far, I haven't went through such any,
But if he'th been trapp'd i' this disposition,
I'd suggest a disqualified disruption,
For he is unfound to disport himself,<50)(M85)
But's disgruntled to collapse by outforce."

Businessman Exits
[CUT/]

(*A view of the hairdresser giving his statement*)

Hairdresser: "Two Monkeys I've born o' Ravioli and Yvon,
In my snicker to hear their last bicker,
Potty talking them, but mention'd of yon,(M85)
A singleness as Ravioli's starter."

Prosecutor: "But i' trait, Ravioli hath laud'd him a starter,
What canst thou remark o' this term?"

Hairdresser: "He assumed,
It as an idiotic symbol that's groom'd,
Of which could be kidd'd by his ignorance."

Prosecutor:"No more Your Honour."

Hairdresser Exits
[CUT/]

(*A view of the Cambodian journalist disclosing Ravioli*)

Cambodian Journalist: "I have befriended Ravioli for years,
Time to time he's ineluctable to hurt
Insistent to annoy his precious slut;
And too, random victims ~ his covenience,
And this man persuad'd, paid—her assailant,
Incontrovertible I could suggest
Amongst his other scapegoats long index'd."

Cambodian Journalist Exits
[CUT/]

[The camera pans] (***Solania forwards an assertion of bail for Jannequin***)
[CUT/]
[The scene is shifted to] (***The judge calls the two lawyers into his chamber***)
[CUT/]
(***A brief view of Jannequin, with his debilitating visage as if burdening a nightmare of how much he would suffer the hanging; or least, the suffering and torture of waiting the death punishment itself.***

The view of Jannequin, and the tumultuous situation in the court room are faded upon the return of the judge, Solania and the prosecutor from the chamber. Solania is viewed shortly, throwing a smiling look at Jannequin. Followingly the judge continues)

Judge: "I' accordance with th' proofs that're deficient
To fortify the accusation 'gainst
The defendant Phillipe Jannequin,
This court hath consider'd wisely to grant
A bail for thee at two thousand ringgits;
But is installed by a term's composite.
I' there's next ev'dence consider'd consequence,
From the fresh successively probe hereon,
The court hath its right to issue a warrant
To retain thee again under Section
Hundred seventeenth of th' Crim'nal Proc'dure Code;
A negative advance notice that's bolt'd.
Till nine o'clock sharp this coming Monday,
This court's now adjourn."

(***Jannequin looks up at the judge. And a moment after exchanging glad observation with Solania***)

EXEUNT

Scene IV (Bukit Bintang & Titiwangsa Lake, Kuala Lumpur)

[A scenery long shot]

(***Poem below is for Choir = Narrator, going through with the screening of mime actions***)

Atop th' firmament, th' fowls've taken their wings,
Th' local detail's bright, meaningful, telling,
Appr'ciation 'long th' J'lan Sultan Ismail,<51) (M86)
Moreo'er hath miniaturised th' peril
O' misery with th' additional vista
Of the sunken sun at the reveria,
Rectitude's joined and remained as a shade
O' indissoluble relationship at th' end o' trade,
E'en strictlier contretemps are there ahead.

[A long shot of] (***a Mazda Astina runs along the Jalan Sultan Ismail***)

[CUT/]

(***Interior of the car,*** [focusing] ***sit Solania and Jannequin. Clad in a tafetta shirt, naught a fancy of a turquoise; Solania's redolent perfume has pervad'd the car's interior. Augmenting Jannequin's attentiveness to study her. Although the trial, is still in the straw that breaks the camel's back, has him not pricked his conscience but remained carefree afterall. Though ever has sat a worriedly thin, he has yet mettled himself and shown a radiant posture.***

Solania decelerates the car as their evening yet warm journey descends at the Scalini's La Piccola Italia restaurant)

[CUT/]

[A close shot of] (***Jannequin and Solania, having a meal of two cups of Coffee Tegoline, and Insalata di polipo con patate e vinogrette alla rucola, of which is an octopus salad with potatoes, vinaigrette sauce and arugola. Dining in peace, while hearkening a jazz song from the restaurant's jukebox; they have their observation oft-thrown at each other***)

[CUT/]

[A close shot with equal panning] (*Jannequin and Solania walk along the Titiwangsa Lake Park. Alive of an unprofligate mirth, they have shared amongst themselves a conversation, while taking their seats on a brick bench*)

4). **Dialogue**

Jannequin: (*cordially praises*)
"Le diner est délicieux, mon Olan, [(F.xii)]
Qui convient à par acquit de conscience;
Ne plus savoir que faire le mien."

Solania: "For a piece of mind?
(*She laughs and adds,*)
"Thou needst more repast, thereon it would conserve
Thy skeletal build, 't goes without saying,
Howsoe'er, I'm putting in a good heading
For thy rejuvenation."

Jannequin: "Thou'rt my phased
Prediliction, my Olan, in the haze,[<52)] [(M87)]
A piecework hath oft-reclaim'd place o' secular
Beneficiary; but thou'rt not any,
'Tis rejoicing my j'yous redundancy.
With this crocodile pouch and a box o' present,
(*He holds firm Solania's hand as he continues,*)
Pray! Favour them thou must as th' prolusion
O' my love."

Solania: "Heaven's certain of my heart, Jannequin,
My affection for thee is long-standing,
E'er outset o' our meeting—benightedly
Is henceforth to-night, reveal'd caringly.
An afterglow of the glorious whisper,
Dour dissipates ire mars—the heart's mantler,
Done justice to its mystique, distrust sear'd
Ingress of love, but like meaning finelier;
Lit upon all the jocundable stars,
I' farrago once but hied myself 'fter task,
As spontaneous 'twas quicken'd a verity
Fast jocundity."

Jannequin: "Olan, loving thee
My highbrow of once and a while keenness,
But i' the fortune at will begone lifeless,
Shalt thou withstand th' supervening surmise?
Lest perhance the case I'm devitalised,
Or r'turn to my nature conspiciously,
The aforesaid beast ere my tongue worthy?"

Solania: "Bemus'd won't 'fter times in th' apple o' discord;
Mark'd heartache but heavy-laden romps' rote, <53) (M88)
Forwent my rootlessable tears adrought,
Though in th' nick of time this life of Riley,
Twice not there'fter me in th' bonds haplessly."

Jannequin: "My truelove, dear Olan, though fresh firmly,(M89)
Grievest thou mustn't i' this night of wonder,
Having a hand in this fecundly pleasure
Once, should be maintained poised evermore.
(***He walks close and kisses her cheek***)
Atop heaven I love thee."

Solania: "Gladly adore
As a jocund woman I am at this height,
Least to say, rejoic'd to this betimes pride."

(***They embrace together in dignified love. While hearts pounding in a rhythm of dove; in a classic verse, they sing their joyness. In the pledge of phrases***)

"Revelation of the Heart" <54) (S.lx)

Sung Verses I (Song) (***7 & 10 syllables***)

(*Jannequin*)

Sough of spirit like blooming chestnut trees,
 Glancing the firmament: drawing prime peace,
I' relation to my grief; aye a vagabond,
 Ennui bow'd my thought, beseeming to mourn;
Drearily eagle with purblind o' lovelorn

Auguring a prize; an archly utterance,
        But mine listing all my expectation,
O! Sweet, my treasure; winning thy rev'rence,
        Into my solely mistress: th' mirth's lantern,
Tying this eminently relation

(***Solania***)

An arcadia shall wash the crow'd humor,
        Where equit'ble love measureless by time,
I kiss th' dourness adieu; all nerves quiver,
        Thy sight my mere might; my glory shall rhyme

When eyes caught eyes, I'm primitively lost,
        Livelong unease; am I worth a value?
But as th' query is answer'd; languor's paus'd,
        Thyself my landmark, a pride my view

<u>Refrain</u> (***Sung together***)

Revelation of the heart,
        Harkens our desire of one,
        Voyaging i' this love expectant, <55) (M90)
        This verily affection,
        Our ventur'd aspiration

Revelation of the heart
This endearment, hands held 'neath,
Ennobling this endow'd mirth,
Heart, mind and soul all be girth'd
By this pristine kiss of love

Instrumental Solo

<u>Sung Verses II</u>

(*Jannequin*)

Pristinely my love, pristinely thy love,
This passionate glory; but sins e'er loath'd,
As satiatedly prance as my heed'd nerve,
Here I conquer thee; but plighting my troth

(*Solania*)

The wrack of light rain from the southeaster,
Trippingly a fortunate peace of nature,
Thy promptly phrases I'm o'erly speechless,
Methought an admiration that's obvious

▬ ▬ ▬

4). **Dialogue**

Jannequin: "*Oui! Merci Olan. Merci! Ma chérie.* <55a) **(F.xiii) (F.xiv)**
To-night, I'm instantly bound to glory."

(*Solania unties the pouch, unwittingly. Surprised and astonished she is with its content; the five round emeralds—fineness their nobility*)

Solania: "Goodness gracious me! Bemused I'm by this,
But, what—"

Jannequin: "These're for thee and our progenies,
Somehow, i' I'd be defeat'd by this trial's glee,
Treat and keep them my bittersweet bequest,
But if the misadventure be chance best'd,
Numbers more o' surprise shall lie beside thee
My truelove."

Solania: (*hugs and persuades Jannequin*)
"'Tis my zealous instinct beholdin'
From th' justifiably tribunal a fervent win,
Upon thy glitter'd guiltless priority,
Though counting chickens ere they're hatch'd fully
Beseeming inadequate; dank daring,
Just, a profit may The Lord glad giving,
Of delightly certitude now, henceforth."

Jannequin: "Thou art but my vital helpmate thus far,
Smiling as this love joint, shall there a herald
Of bliss in th' ascendant o' all thy travails."

Solania: "Hmm."
(*She answers soft while reclining her head unto his chest*)

(***Poem below is for Choir = Narrator or Musical Accompaniment to the screened action***)

As night dissolves and the smiling sun o' morn
Hath waken the next day; venture to vaunt,
But e'en as the habitués o' th' garden
Hav' gradually arriv'd; num'rous vision,
The two observ'd lovers are still sleeping.
Pate met pate, hands held hands; ever throwing
Themselves down in th' phantasy of one dream,
Begon'd astray in th' arcane '*fondness stream*'.

EXEUNT

Scene V (A) (The Criminal Section Court II, Jalan Raja, Kuala Lumpur)

(***Poem below is for Solania <u>or</u> Musical Accompaniment to the screened action <u>or</u> both***)<56)

'Regular changes of weather a cinch,
In its fix'd cycle, sufferable, tense,
Authoris'd by revolution of th' tides;
Rain, tempest, hotness—felt naturally.
'Twas th' twentieth day of the critical trial,
Bending an ear to deceitful witness's,
Or the obtrud'd evidence from research,
Constrain'd Jannequin to th' 'stant consternation."

(*Within this poem read by Solania, [we have a long shot of] a police inspector, DSP Zaid, giving a factual admittance to the court, of which could 'logically' proves Jannequin's guilt. [This scene is then faded to] Another witness, Madeina, a friend of Yvon; providing her statement against Jannequin*)

5A). **Dialogue**

Madeina: "I'm close to Yvon but I sob her dear choice,
Snazzy and snooty barons her precious,
Snuffling her romances like grown mushrooms,
But they're yet skiv'd brats including this man."

Prosecutor: "Thou hath report'd to notice his misdemeanour,
Pray reexpose them to court."

Madeina: "I'd harkened earlier;
Three nights ere the ignoble planned murder,
Yvon had said not singular with this man,
She'd mind'd to befriend him but i' incubus
Apprehend'd one of Ravioli's conspirators."

Solania: "Whence did Yvon detect this feas'ble message?"

Madeina: "When this man had telephon'd and quoth'd,
'I'm not venturesome to guard a harlot,
For they mere merit'd cold exaltation;
At open sward I'd hav' lewd dominion.'"(M92)

(*The court turns chaotic for a moment.* [A long shot of] ***A man spectator rises***)<57)

Spectator: "She's very skulduggery!"

Judge: (*bangs his gavel in few knocks*) "Pray silent!"
Pray silent! Salute the rules of this court.
(*The court laughs*)
"Many are blind sages; a misconception,
Pray extend thy statements Miss Madeina."

Madeina: "She told me to hide her somewhere,
I urged my man to help but mis'rably
We've miscalculated th' capture o' Yvon."

Madeina Exits

[CUT/]

(*Rise three university students, carrying the genuine verity of the murder*. [The camera is pulled back to take a brief close shot of] *Jannequin's visage is seriously convoluted; while Solania's voice is heard reading the poem below*:)

'Though gruelling a fight, but when fashion's right
Is aye correctly hand'd as souvenir,
As dazzling as his star i' hugger-mugger;
And th' fortunate love 'tween us had alight,
Had carri'd th' world ere us that soulful tide.'

[Meanwhile, a long shot of] (*The three students are discussing with each other in the witness box*)

[CUT/]

[The camera pans] (*Solania ambles near the students while glancing at the court, and thereafter a moment, faces the judge*)

Solania: "Your Honour, here I'd like to represent
Another witnesses of whom've spectat'd
The event on the night of the killing."

Judge: "'Tis a commendable significance,
Worth'd an impressive consideration."
(***The court is again brought to laughter***)

A Woman Spectator: "Be not in featherweight o' information,
My instinct saith he's not the chosen guilt,
Pray make him wisefully released."

A Punk Boy: "Hey men!
Give this court a kick of verity."

Judge: "Pray silent!
Th' law hates much extended, non preferential noise.
(***While he bangs his gavel twice on the bench , the court is again brought to a short chuckle. The judge addresses the students***)
"Y'art earnest to utter at once?"

Marzipan, Bahrin & Gerard: "Yea Your Honour!"

Solania: "Mister Marzipan and thy familiars,
Aren't ye still schooling?"

Marzipan, Bahrin & Gerard: "Yea we are madam!"

Marzipan: (***elongates dodderily while trying to comfort himself***)
"Third year students o' pharmaceutical course
At the University o' Malaya."

Solania: "Mister Marzipan, what canst thou describe
Th' exactness o' th' scenes? Can start from outset."

Bahrin: "We were on foot to a classmate's dwelling,
Occassionally had pass'd this area."

EXEUNT

Scene V (B) (Jalan Stonor, Kuala Lumpur)

(***Continues Gerard's voice while [the camera takes a long shot of] a yellow Proton Iswara, brakes nearby a lamppost***)

"''Twas close nine fifteen night, suddenly lied
On the way; about thirty feet ahead,
Pervert'dly supervening our journey,
And obsess'd our interest, anxiety.
Aware o' th' danger of which might befall
We obnoxiously hid in a covert,
Hard by the parked car; breathless curt,
Obviously a horrid scene, under the light,
We'd prick'd up our ears till 'twas all over.
The strangers we'd harked; a mem'ry's agape,(<58) (M93)
Were Ravioli, Hussein and Oxenville.
Th' shiver unseen for she was lying s'pine (M94)
And head cover'd.'

5B). **Dialogue**

Oxenville: “Joyous evil have made
Us all cuddled by pleasure that’s sedate,
Culminating with wetness. Ha! Ha! Ha!”

Yvon: (*Unseen from the screen*) “Ne’er! Nay!”

Hussein: “Twee the skin. Give it a tweak, now!”

Yvon: “Nay! Aaah!”

Ravioli: “This’s my turbidity, Yvon; from thy hate,
Quoth thee a twaddle—is now fairly paid.”

(***Marzipan’s voice is heard as the*** [camera passes shots between] ***the students and the blurred underrated scenario carries on***)

‘Tho’ obscene but ‘twas a pity afterall,
Insupportably had the scared victim,
She was developed to be ravish’d raw,
Tighten’d and scream’d but constrict’d till soundless.
If perchance she might hav’ collaps’d awhile;
Like th’ harken’d death’s shout ere was gunn’d lifeless.
‘Twas unobliged for us to react an aid,
For had passively awestruck by the gun,
Our baleful contretemps.’

(***Then Bahrin’s voice*** [while the camera pans] ***describes the acts of the three criminals — Ravioli, Oxenville, and Hussein respectively***)

'The three villains
I' brevity thenceforth, had a quaint discussion
Of another hot plan.'

5B). **Dialogue** [59]

Oxenville: "Hey! Harken me all men!
This point o' meeting's to save because I am
Bland with a baloney.[M95] Hold! She is damn'd
And full our gratification, but not our hope."

Hussein: "Relax th' awry bone or marred by gloat'd globe,[M96]
This pleasure is poison and poison's bait."

Ravioli: "Detach thy worryguts and battle fright,
The conceit I hold's a bamboozling toss
Against th' absent-mind'd Jannequin. See close?"

Oxenville: "Certifying our certitude. Then what?"

Ravioli: "I'll pinprick him slowly with fuddling treat,
With pills of Ephedrine and priced cocktail,
Dose him be cloyed to snake sleep; airs, graces,
And send him here; a mere clue o' this business."

Oxenville: "Damn! Damn thee clumsy."

Ravioli: "The cockle is used
With a tall concealment."

EXEUNT

Scene V (C) (In the Courtroom, Jalan Raja, Kuala Lumpur)

5C). **Dialogue**

Marzipan: "When they'd lost from sight, we'd just left the place,
Discourag'd to study th' disgusting corse,
Till this last Monday when we heard his trial,
We'd decided to assert the statement."

(*Thunderous claps are heard from the court*)

Solania: "Thanks for the important piece o' evidence,
Misters Gerard, Bahrin and Marzipan."

Gerard, Bahrin and Marzipan Exit

(*Solania smiles and turns toward the judge*)
"Your Honour. From these endorsed witnesses
I could position the prior stated proof,
That my client is not guilty as accused,
But's used mere a target of maltreatment."

Judge: "I see the profusion o' strong probity.
Any other view from th' prosecutor?"

Prosecutor: "Nay Your Honour. Th' probity's signatured."

Judge: "The production of this law is not blind."
(*A short laughter from the court*)
"This court hath made its judgment to acquit
All th' charges against Mister Jannequin,
As th' felony o' th' murder of malice
Aforethought on the victim—Yvon Laurel;
This case is hereupon, dismissed."

(*The judge knocks his gavel once on the bench while smiling at Jannequin and Solania*)

[CUT/]

[A Close Shot of] (***Jannequin embraces Solania, tightly in love and exaltation for the success. Avers the judge*** [as the camera turns toward him] ***before leaving***)

Judge: May The Creator blessest ye together
Unto thine everlasting harmony."

Solania & Jannequin: "Thanks thee with priority Your Honour."

Judge, Prosecutor Exit

[CUT/]

[A view of] (***The exterior of the court. Few anxious photographers and journalists are rushing after Jannequin.*** [The camera pans] ***Jannequin and Solania answer the journalists shortly while proceeding into Solania's Mazda***)

5C). **Dialogue**

Journalist I: "What's thy respect with the peevish matter?"

Jannequin: "Methought it is the prissy privation,
And a principle to break a random greeting
Anon i' my hilarity."

Journalist II: "Probably,
What are you going to do next?"

Jannequin: "Building
A mansion and thereafter wed my Solania—
My tempted lobelia."

EXEUNT

Scene VI (The Court Compound & Tun Dr Ismail Garden, Damansara)

(***Poem is for Choir = Narrator <u>or</u> Solania and Jannequin mimed action, except the song Honey is for Jannequin***)

Nimble 'mag'nation withdraws negligence,
Infirmity o' purpose not in askance,
Nine days wonder the victory beseems,
Screens of mirth are expand'd; hymeneal deems
Shine the shiningly lamps; enthrall the night,
Enrapture all hearts with 'normous[(M98)] dinner,
Ensemble o' sonata e'nobles [(M98)] her pride,[<61)]
Vivac'ty revamps heart; luck to finger

Farce with its concomittant jocos'ty,
A consequent of leisure but not vain,
Confound'd by wedding's gift touching glory;
The joyous mansion of him; his love main,
Princely his treat; her Halycon days r'main'd

Wedding's rejoiced by vantage's familiars,
I' a crowd o' aristocratic proprietors,
Honeymoon—mantled by jocund dom'nance,
Her mere dreamland ~ this newly residence;
And his hymned free verse she's hush'dly entranc'd

Jannequin:

Honey <61a) (S.x)

(iFAN Music & Art W.042)

Sung 1st Verses (Song) [*Free Verse or Prose*]

Honey, to wherever the destiny,
E'en... to nowhere the end might be,
You and I still be strong
To meet and challenge... this life together

Honey, whatsoever our history,
It is just our past story
This life we've shared, for a longlong time,
May soon turn bright as gold

Refrain

In this brink of fragrance,
        Bring us a field of flower,
Through the morning mist
        Here to us with wonder

In the range of our reach,
        They stay oh! O-hooo!
This eternal-sweet-true love

Sung 2nd Verses

Honey, as I've fixed in my promise,
Those uncertainties would never strike us
Again, but... a replacement
Of satiation

Honey, i' this everlasting harmony,
Also both we hope the same as us
Happen... to the rest of them [**Repeat Chorus**]

▬ ▬ ▬

(*Poem is for Choir = Narrator* ***or*** *Solania and Jannequin mimed action*)

Might is in call; lost deep-seated sorrow,
Hath mock'd evil's tendency; smirk'd its wise,
Terpsichorean mode's joy'd in; like a rill's flow,
Love be brought to retire, 'ffair's concise;
Astir later 'nother to mesmerise

As good as his words; certain as a gold rush,
A goodly business — a grandly hotel;
Harken'd glamour: a well-spring like a spell,
A hypnotist; hero worship o' him her hush,
The wealth, he saith, her sat'd smile to compel

At the drop of a hat; standing her ground,
Letter o’ resignation seals her r’tirement,
Rev’vified by th’ Estima; a vaunt to count,
But the adieu’s gift of hugg’d love to sound;
The laughter ere hath declin’dto lament

Immortalising a man’s thought o’ his mode,
A belov’d figure of him brave must his loss,
Th’ ‘e’erlasting harm’ny’, lost!; ashens each nod,
By and by ardour d’partured mal’dy ‘bode; (M99) <62)
Abed nay o’ late ‘xalt’tion; somn’lence enforc’s

For all the worlde, humbleness turns luckless,
Tasting strychnine but hence must be swallow’d,
The sorrowing moments his pride i’ tatters;
Spake touching his provenance—her stopp’d tears,
By heavyhearted wave she is wallow’d

[A Long Shot of] (***The beautiful bungalow and its surroundings. The night is airily cold, with liliputian drops of rain befriending the bungalow***)

[CUT/]

[A Close Shot of] (***Solania and Jannequin, closely sit at the veranda ~ giving their souls to be buoyed by the dismally atmosphere. Few times he glances at her; intendedly a secret study on the feature of his sorely admiration.***

He knows the beast energy in him is marring his human structure. The mark of truth has outlined his estimation as his touch on the glass is beyond his normal realisation; a certainty to be wild is within doubtless, thenceforth. Yet difficult to agree, he tries hard to gulp the red chianti)

6). **Dialogue**

Jannequin: "Olan, nobuild shall kick th' bucket with th' drink,
My convenience's, aheight, atop to grin;
Anon shall boisterous glory betide."
(***Propitiates him as he tries to withdraw Solania's disheartenment. Solania bewails; cheeks bedewed with tears***)

Solania: "Jannequin, wherefore this malady robs
Thy pristinely build? My rocky heart throbs,
Art thou not loving me as much as ere?"

Jannequin: "Olan.
(***He takes her hand and kisses it***)
"My heart hath clove to thine till devil's shunn'd,
Ne'er this kingdom o' love best'd by obstacles;
Quench th' existence o' my solid 'spect tho' death shall,
But my spirit'th ne'er begone even fell
From thy spirit and thy world."

Solania: "But vain all
This glory along with thy departure.
Together with my measureless pleasure
Shall scythe all my vigour."

Jannequin: "Nay Olan! Nay!
Not this I laud much o' thine act. Olan, pray!

Solania: "I' lifeless's measur'd as the eternal mirth,
I'm i' 'lysium departing from this lone earth."

Jannequin: "Olan! Th' aforesaid death's not meant lifeless,
Apprehendest thou must."

Solania: "Therefore what else
Jannequin? Are not there another tales
Be screen'd in words? Or phantasized ver'ty
That's trivially reject'd?"

Jannequin: "This phantasy
Is priced not as low as that rejection."
(***He coughs—a senile cough***)

Solania: "If 'tis not that low then apace explain,
Pray my love, explain it!"

(***Solania strains her head against his laps; whimpering like a child, but in her displeasure. He mildly kisses her temple.*** [An EFX view of the slow transformation of] ***Jannequin changes to the skull of an eagle, while he sings the Cavatina*** **(S.xi)** ***below***)

Jannequin: "Craving for wisdom touch not its answer,
Give much credence I won't to this 'mergence,
But hath ach'd numbly protest as a heir,
'Cme[M100] a fowl; measureless journey i' imminence,
'Cquaint'd [M100] th' firmament ignores olden grievance,[<63]
Immat'rial puts to imb'cile[M101]; eyes sore, blur,
Idiosyncrasy then paints the soul mere;
Spirit shrinks below midget—intense's clott'd,
Bloom a man hath descend'd; fort'tude beseems naught,
Bloom an eagle impassive befriended;
For th' imp'rially pinion's much coveted,
Kisser in lather transforms into beak,
Visage shrinks unto a skull; latitude'speak'd,
Plumage materialises the shape's course,[M102]
Legs in transition into sharpen'd claws.
Pinion demolishes the hands; time's purs'd,[M103]
Preying fowl its kingdom; thews o' wilderness,
Taking wing heaven forth, heartache thicker,
And, remains e'erlastingly in th' humor.
Left all trueloves afar behind; grey th' hue,
Merely left a passionate fowl-eye view
Of the olden mirth's sorely vehement.
But as misadventure's there to return,
Retrovertion hence listed by notion;
Actuality but is felt nevermore.

(*Solania has fallen asleep. But Jannequin still continues,*)

"Here th' verity thus put to faint by lime,
But pray! Urging thee on this figured time,
Bring forth my progenies; the moulds of me,
My spirit their spirits tho' odd it might be,
My conscience their conscienc's; intent nay 'vil,
My being their beings; instill'd noble,
But, my treble incubus are not theirs,
And, my ill-fat'd revolution, I'm th' last.
Singularity haply thy mere woe,
Howsoe'er, my departure—them in th' row
I' replacement; exalt'tion blossoms thee i' throng,
Golds in all daylong, diamonds i' all nightlong,
Th' charisma i' me that thou hath laud'd freely,
Marred not and shall be a bournless pride of me;
Marred ne'er but too a bournless pride of thee.
O! The night is falling, morn is calling,
Time begone apace, my freedom's ending
Bowing the urge unto this sorrowing
Departure."

(Jannequin lays her on the bed. His magical verses has entirely dosed Solania. And together his formation has worsened. Merely a skull of a bald eagle replaces his visage. Awhile waiting for the time, he writes down a poem (r. Act II, Scene 3:refer par.16). *As the clock on the wall strikes sharp at four o'clock, he is shaped fully a bald eagle. Trippingly a movement of a natural fowl; taking wing in an unease, it leaves the place solemnly. Leaving as a memorial behind—its few plumage*)

Jannequin/Eagle Exits
[CUT/]

(*When the cockcrow opens the dawn, Solania sits on the swivel chair—shedding tears. She crumples the paper (which contains the poem); singing there alone in forlorn*)

Solania:

'Thy Love' <63a) **(S.xii)**
(iFAN Music & Art W.013)

Sung Verses I & II (Song) [*Free Verse*]
At the betimes morn
Thou left me; hermit
In lovelorn,
Laughter sunken'd
Into shades; coldly,
Quick me in despondency

Purblindness
Displeases me;
Mirth's now bootless,
But our glorious memory
E'ermore a mate fast to me

Pre-Refrain I & II:

Livelong day in unease,
Nightfall—insipidness tease,
Naught to befriend; Alas!
These thy gifts
A remembrance,
In all my tears

Refrain:

Thy love
E'ermore here with me,
Thy love
Lit up wonder and glory

Thy love
Made my dreams came true,
I shall keep thy words
Till the tide of quietus;
Where is my end

(***The poem below is for Solania as the scene fades into darkness***)

'At long last; fortnightly I was tied in woe,
At that same place; the unyielding tam'd chair,
I join'd my quotidian life, thereafter.
Business, contracted by measured schedule
To me at a time; like a red flag to a bull,
Tho' desperation of this misfortune
Burnt in my squeez'd heart; like-mindedness tun'd,
And here ~ ailing health is revived.'

'Eagle & Th' 5 Eggs' — Part I, ACTS I, II, & III – 8:47AM 19/11/2021

Part II
(ACTS IV & V)

(This division is for the convenience of actors to memorise the long verses for staged opera, TV Opera, or long Play Film.

- Firadyanié 1998)

Eagle and th' Fiv' Eggs

(5 Acts Comically Operatic Play/Film)
(W.104 of Ido Firadyanié Art Nouveau Collections)

ACT IV

Scene I (Tun Dr Ismail Garden, Damansara)

olania weeps under Ljiljana's embrace. Tears, in a string of beads [as the camera is withdrawn to focus Caesarea] is seen coursing his cheeks; taking pity to Solania's woe. Although the accompaniment to her song, 'Thy Love' has over, Caesarea still plays the piano.

[CUT/]

[A scene of the bungalow's surrounding] (***'Tis nearing eventide, but the shaded wall has presumed a crepuscularly scene. Striking the last note below pianissimo*** [a close shot, at a low angle of, Caesarea's fingers and the piano, and as he allots his sense to Jannequin's portrait, the camera also takes a brief shot of the portrait]. ***Here is to give a meaning that Caesarea is joining with his personal feeling for a moment***)

1). **Dialogue**

Caesarea: (*tries to allay Solania*)
"Sister, allegiance haply thou'th shown,
Also th' amazement through time as well scenes,
But thenceforth o'er head and ears it'd begone;
Simplic'ty untold hardship unexplain'd,
Every thine olden mirth sears;
A fell dreariness. Yet to bear—
The scarr'd confidence and jocundity.
I cry as my slipp'd words fly,

Though witticisms I'd try,
But the profuse laughter this wouldn't help,
Pronounc'd just a propensity of crap;
In capitulation against dismay,
Significant, I'm cannilier not say,
Thus candidness shouldn't frust."

Solania: "Nay Aria!."
Pray! As thou mayst."

Caesarea:

"Captive Don't by Deploration" (64) (S.xiii)

(A Scena. If Aria—Aria all'unisono. Choir on the refrain and no repetition)
[8 & 10 syllables]

Sung Verses

A history, if accurate my psyche,
    Descent entrance, orally mouth to mouth,
A dependable knowledge not archaic,
    Life of a chagriner—personal's bough (MI04)

Fanning himself the sole capitalist, (MI05)
    Iron hot of substance; (MI05) irasciblier,
Ipso facto an irrationalist, (MI05)
    Involved, inviolable stance to revere

Unsolicit'd chuckl'd; hot comes raine comes,
Unvarnish'dly 'dores cigar repast charms,
One day another, slump turns poverty, <65) (M106)
With full kins to heaven he was gloomy

Untidiable, smouldered by verity,
Unthinkable—oft-cri'd wanes mastery
Trembl'd his brain not lesson; jaded fast,
Cold favour, tatter'd shirts clad in at last

Warrantable he went then an ancient,
Unstinting 'dvice, sagely viewpoint's certain,
Utter'd soft, pric'd gentle, meaning radiant,
Th' chagriner's assurance quot'd recurrent

Set 1 Refrain

Captive don't by deploration, (M107)
What's taken as what is given,
A portion limited by its Creator,
Tho' felt and damn'd for all loss,
Verily done but wicked none,
But an apprehension a must—most
'Tis a patience's test to confront

Captive don't by deploration,
What is left is what is to care,
Tho' unpalatable hath the smile,
But piousness must not impair,
When 'ther bliss could be compil'd
Covering days pass'd in bile

Set 2 Refrain

Captive don't by deploration,
What's the past as what is the last,
Tho' olden speech's are upheld robust;
Naught a humble fault but soppy boast,
Thus a misery be not misconstru'd;
Or furthest an anathema,
But mystic'lly offers grandeur
For the periods of afterlife

Captive don't by deploration,
What is a world is mere a world,
As its fame merely temporal,
Tho' some saith a Ruritanian pleasure,
But in delirium the quickly nature;
Just, this denot'd demarcation
Shouldn't actual mean to demean,
Again yet spoken and spoken,

As lasting as a Holy Hymn,
But a must an apprehension,
'Tis a patience's test to confront

▬ ▬ ▬

Caesarea: (*continues*) "Sister,
Vulnerable is not a sturdy standing; (M109) <67)
For thine anorexia is now ruling,
Forasmuch as I'm concreting concern,
That I'm listing the new youngs' attendance;
Eavesdropping, but wakeful still they don't come,
O! Sister, sorry. I've botch'd up thee."

Solania: "Nay Aria.
Nay nay. Comest thou into my embrace."

(***Caesarea hugs Solania tight. Ljiljana, Solania and Caesarea are buoyed in tears. Then, a sound of bird's chirp comes within them***)

[CUT/]

[A brief shot of] (***On the slumber's bed, the eaglets have just hatched***]

Fiv' Eaglets: 'Tweet! Tweet! Tweet!'

[CUT/]

[A shot of] (***Caesarea, Ljiljana and Solania in their short suspicious silence***)

Caesarea: "I'm bath'd by my acme of assumption. (M110)
Sister, mother, metell ye. They are coming,
Again, hark their interesting noise!"

Fiv' Eaglets: 'Tweet! Tweet! Tweet!'

Solania: (*affirms while wiping her tears*)
"Tempting my hearing; thus—*je ne sais quoi*." <68) **(F.xv)**

Caesarea: "I'm tensing up. Counting a find a pleasure,
For meknow an egg crashes once."

Ljiljana: "Aria.
(*She utters in an unsavoury scintilla*)
"I counsel, thriving with thine excitement
Not (M111) during this period o' thy sister's pain,
As Church's bell summon to Christian custom;
Wise the cry o' worship from the minaret—
One after all our frame of reference,
Thus move on and invoke."

Caesarea: "Yea Mama yea!
'Tshall be stapled inside my routine discipline."
(*As he runs upstairs* [off-screen], *Ljiljana and Solania laugh at him*)

[CUT/]

[The camera pans] (*Caesarea while stopping midway, utters the scroll content*)

"A coxcomb forsooth verbally welly wott'd,
But a benign stripling o' but proudless deed,
A treasure to hope and laud; fervent hot,
Though of bestial ancestry; least heed."

(***As a clever codicil, Caesarea adds his:***)
Practical, nine to six, normal job hours,
While M.S.C.[(M112)] world of future powers,[<69)]
Witness hourglass, grand still hath this old pride,
But to me a jockey's card to excite

Demurely eagle, I file my fatigue
When I am craving for a doze's brig,
Durable still I say for bloom of self,
Thy youngs—bestial moulds of iron delft."

Fiv' Eaglets: 'Tweet! Tweet! Tweet!'

Caesarea: "Nah! Right! The spirits of the iron delfts
Are asking but my rapid attendance;
Vainliness not rare for mine—a slow coach."

(***Caesarea enters the room. His surprise overrules his manner***)

[CUT/]

[A close shot to where he looks] (***The bed, once methodically arranged in it beauty, is faded with droppings. The fiv' eaglets are pointing their visions at Caesarea.*** [The camera is now shifted back to focus] ***Caesarea in a still wonderment***)

"I'm speechless with my sight. Delight's feedback;
Y'art a present o' laughter. Sister! Mama!
Apace o'er here. Be immediate if could!

(***He replaces all the eaglets in a fish box, found to be emptied and practically clean . While sitting, he studies them***)

"Malacca, Parameswara's treasure;
And a court, parachut'd from paradise,
Denoting his majesty—his pleasure.
But thy pater a Parisian; a man a disguise,
Pathos ~ hath return'd atop firmament,
During the moon o' goat as per Gregorian,
I watch but thou smilest a nestling smile,
And thy mater sure lessened her distress' pile,
Behold! Their clinging footsteps are now fast."

Ljiljana: (***enters whilst pushing Solania's wheelchair***)
"I'm downright shock'd. Scenting live marionettes,
Sensational figures, lass. They are great!"

(***Solania forces her wheel chair forward. She comes close to the box. Holding one of the eaglets in her admiration, speaks her motherly vehemence***)

Solania: "Ye, thy father's spirits. I'm speaking posh
When a mother's forever a mother;
Just lucid—I'm lib'ralis'd, lenient,
And my liking is most everything,
And is customis'd with this emergence,
Insulting I would not; ye my children,
Assuredly I am not turning a hair,

When assert'd implausible to impair;
Though... perceptively this isn't a perfection.
But, I'm not viewing a perfectionist
Though my time's e'ermore spent querulous,
And mere hating myself not loving ye,
But to this love's—insensibility,
Obtruded—I'm without anomaly
Mother's waft."(M114)

EXEUNT

Scene II (Same Place)(<71)

(***The cloudy atmosphere is pressurising lopsided veneration for its onlookers; sympathising either rain or heeded hotness. [A close shot] While the indistinct presentation has been still a spectacle for Caesarea, he runs his cunning hands, oversizing the parrot's cage. Mainly a steel framework of welded-joint iron bars, the construction is within endmost. The parrot's has been substituted with a wooden birdcage at the backyard***)

[CUT/]

[A long shot of] (***Mister Ashraf's wife, Siti Jana—the neighbour*** (r. Act I, Scene I), ***is seemed ravished to meet Caesarea again; at the moment she notices Caesarea on the spot***)

2). **Dialogue (A)**

Siti Jana: "Huu! Hello! Mister Caesarea...
Hello! Hoo! Am I out for doubtful o' name's
Gravity? But memento's common blind,
Huu! Hello! Mister Caesarea—"

(*Albeit the weighted weld's scratch, the last vociferation by Siti Jana thereafter, could be scarcely caught by Caesarea. The preference to be warmed by the surroundings is therefore engulfed by his asymmetric fuss. Retraced and found—the direction of the calling, he nervously smiles at Siti Jana. Putting his best foot forward, he replies*)

Caesarea: "I am conscience-striken madam,
The noise's overamplified here.
How long... err thou'rt?"

Siti Jana: "Haven't conjectured
My configuration?(M115) Consenting old colour—
Siti Jana?"(72)

Caesarea: "I'm scarcely dislodging
My motive weight if emended error's
Fitly, thou art Haji Ashraf 'swife."

Siti Jana: "There art thou!
(*She smiles with empathy*)
The covey on the air, deftable flair;
And when pessimism won't help survive,
They're even still warbling—airily fair,
When th' warring cloud don't sigh; emotive knife,
A sightseer shall treat this a dumbly fatigue,
But the cowboy the hot Troy—this's a kick,

Haply, I mind not any of its prick,
As I treat and mend domestic crux weak,
Ah! Naught a notion, I'm culturedly bleak,
And therefore culminating the topic,
How long have you been here?"

Caesarea: "My sense hath favour'd
Thy verse madam. Crystal clear a period
Six moons till this triumph."

Siti Jana: "Hath not thou born
A featured relation with this full-grown
Householder? Err Solania isn't she?"

Caesarea: "Twice yea. The relevance is held by thee;
Social perception irrespectively,
She is finely my adopted sister,
Sight philia, I am adored a great brother—
Forsoothly. Insular a tale to narrate,
But to stay here I'm felicitous rat'd."

Siti Jana: "Straightforward innate thankfulness thou art.
With witticism spake a humble kisser,
A mystical glory to share and bear,
A mainspring for broadable relation,
Howsoe'er th' sister; none self-obtrusion,
Merely not ease identified a feature

Amongst the cautiously civilians here,
Viz a statue of leisurely neglect,
While her logic's social beseems nay track,
Less perchance it is her passivity
For any sort of sociability.
How's she now?"

Caesarea: "My constant sympathy sobs,
Her malady is still solidified,
I'm wishing her fussed woe doesn't broaden."

Siti Jana: "What a prickly fissure she is inside.
Hasn't she been brought for special treatment
Ever yet?"

Caesarea: "The latter-day medical
Proficiency is a digression o' valuable aid,
A transience if could be a percept
Drily and tentatively the answer.
(***He replies unsavourily. Changing his concern:***)
Is Mister Ashraf well-favour'dly formative
After all?"

Siti Jana: "As th' cigar's smoke's inhaler
Inviting cancer but's still addictive,
And later hath his pain solidified.
(***She has then repeated her meddlesome query***)
"Thou art tediously with that building work,
What 'tis supposed to be?"

Caesarea: "Aha! This program's
For my pet's chief aviary. And forsooth
Five eagle's youngs."

Siti Jana: "Eaglets?!"

Caesarea: "The cheery truth."

Siti Jana: "That is by itself a self-joke esteem.
Where didst thou find 'em?"

Caesarea: "A distant familiar;
Abridged ~ partly business partly scholar,
Hath regaled me with this gift—a connexion
With profit as to pinpoint."

Siti Jana: "Hath not thou named them?"
Caesarea: "Umm! Neither in my frame of thought(M117) yet." <74)

[Off-screen] (***Afar, at the demand of attention from his dwelling ~ Mr Ashraf vociferates***)

Mr Ashraf: "JANA!

Siti Jana: "Ouch! Oh. Shocks me all out."

Mr Ashraf: (***aside continues***) "Thy vogue queries shall eat much the previous
Concentration. Th' regulat'd rec'pe first
Is hanging midway its head completion.
This world'll not last today; th' preparation
Is gunning thyself now!"

Siti Jana: “What a captious radiance
Jolting my conscience?
(***Grumbles her but continues,***)
“Young developer, my work is requesting me;
Putting me at a gallop. A custom cutely.
Er! If vacant thy pastime, just spend a bit
Of it at my house.”

Caesarea: “Sure! Gladly and pleased.
Th’ saviour taste o’ thy previous dinner still tempts,
Thus take thy pace with awareness madam,
The path may be slippery.”

Siti Jana Exits

(***Progressing his work after Siti Jana is out of sight, Caesarea smiles alone at her farcical character. Another ring of attraction is a postman’s short tune, while entering the house’s compound with a bunch of letters. The postman’s harmonica sets its introduction***)

Postman:

‘Posthaste Postie’ <74a) (S.xiv)

Sung Verses (*Song; Mixed 4, 7 & 8 syllables*)

The delivery’s express,
        Distance spake pretentiousness,
When prevalence do not stress,
        Apple o’ discord i’ vainliness

The orders the needs nay base,
        This machine—steel dog o' burthen;
To the doors—a good a mission,
        Sometimes hassles a grimace
When a goliath the pattern

<u>Refrain</u>

Posthaste postie,
  I breathe my glee,
And pigeon-chest'd;
Though is pig-head'd
When a cust'mer's mad

Posthaste postie,
  I' view i' vim to be
This violet smile,
But don't beguile,
Dislike be spoilt

Posthaste postie,
Earn me moneys,
Some saith I'm good,
Some saith I'm rude,
Op'd not to dispute

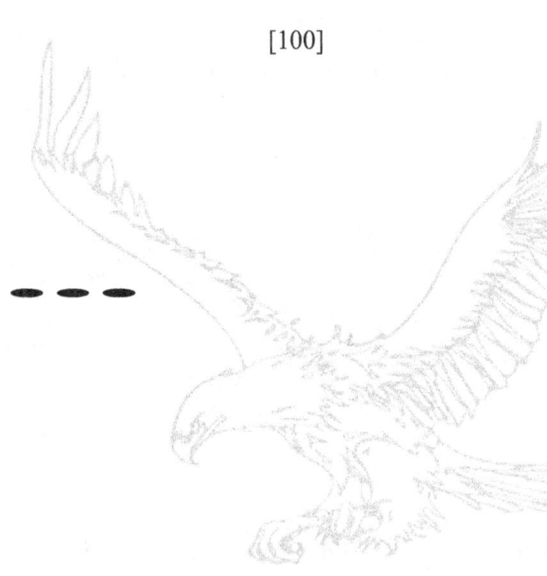

2). **Dialogue (B)**

Caesarea: “Man, I presume this
If crackpot’s heavy—a coltish colour,
But if the revolt stands venturesomely,
Try not exuding, for peace wants thee.”

Postman: “Aye
Sir, I appreciate it. Mere I’m wide-eyed
To the nauseous motivator.”

Caesarea: “If you don’t mind
Having a cup of coffee here?”

Postman: “O! Thanks.
Ere e’entide I’ve to end my del’very.
Haply another day puts my break on
To greet th’ invitation—fulfilled aeon.”
(*Smiles the postman while reversing his motorcycle*)

Solanla: (*calls* [while appearing on the screen]. *She pushes the wheelchair herself into the garden*)
“Aria, what’s up there?”

Postman: “Please thy luxurious noon ma’am.”
(*Politely greets the postman*)

Caesarea: "Sister, I'm enjoying his tuneful verse,
Melodious till alighting my warmness."

Solania: "Fortunately I heard it a little.
By the way, have a luncheon here, mister."

Postman: "Thank you twice, next time shall it be nicer."
(***Apacely he leaves*** [off-camera])

Postman Exits

Caesarea: "What a man."

Solania: "Aria, th' very next hour
Is favour repasts my dear.
Apprehended I'm with this,
A hobby o' thee; the praised work,
But be roasted not till crease
Thy might; for this's mock-up lurk'd,<75)(M118)
Where calling my major wish
When this's not a malformation;
When 't looks unp'reil an event,
Here marked its completion."

Caesarea: "Methink not quite.
(***He gives all the letters to Solania***)
The finest product's a choice o' my conscience."

Solania: "Eh? An eyewash; drawing on my passion,
Wouldst thou pray read it for me?"

Caesarea: (*utters the short address while tearing the envelope*)
"'My lobelia, mere my revered Olan.'

(*The letter's content is written in a verse passage*)
Dear,

Losing mettle; th' dismay o' th' welkin,
Hath pressurised me to call a familiar,
Whom thus versed of fountain pen; a man I mean,
Whom thus pronounced, at will, my desire;
A malleable manservant, dimming my fear,
And I've prospect'd th' second man; a stripling, Caesarea—
mannerism his virtue,
And I knew my wonders, thus in'tiating,
Where in my boon I shall name our bloods new:
Solace—first daughter,
Lovepress—next daughter,
Amethyst—first son,
Nixloath—second son, Antidoubt—
third son.
Tho' by intellect, a singular concept,
But I deny not thy will and adapt.
Olan, I'm taking wing north late to-night,
Haply a week more shall in homeward glide,
Watch my emergence during next hours

On th' point o' thy rooftop; one o' alit towers.
I'm cyanide poisoned i' my forlorn curst,
With thy malady so distress to nurse,
But evaporated ne'er through my hope,
Thy recovery, smile, laughter—the scope.
Olan, livest thou for me,
Thee, th' generator o' my next might.

Thy Truelove

Solania: "O! Jannequin." (***She sobs***)

Caesarea: "Sister, pray! Lacerate nay more thine anxiety."

(***Fast to out of breath, Solania whispers to him***)
Solania: "Aria, couldst thou catch my tongue?"

Caesarea: "Sister,
Yea yea. Pray control thyself."

Solania: "To..ge..ther
Add.. behind.. those.. names,
(***She utters breathlessly,***)
"Solace... the Compass,
Lovepress... the West, then... Amethyst... the East,
Nixloath... the North, and... Antidoubt... the South.
(**Monologue**) My Jannequin, wherefore thy love is short
In my adoration? 'S it not gawky
For a spartan sorry? I'm.. I'm insist'd
To death upon this all."

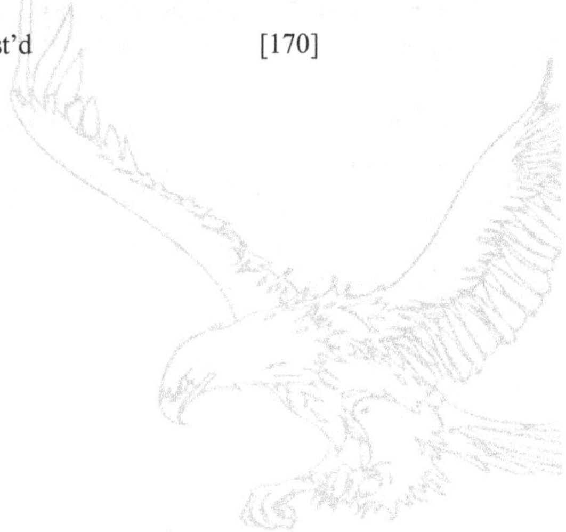

Caesarea: “Sister! Naay!
Mama! Come over here!”

(***The old woman runs*** [into the screen] ***and helps Caesarea***)
Ljiljana: “O my good Lord!
How did this all happen Aria?!”

Caesarea: “I am...
I’m shifting without my conceit, [MT19] (<76)
An explanation is a fuss now.
I must call for an aid.”

[The camera pans] (***Caesarea carries Solania and lays her on the sofa at the hall. Followingly, he telephones her personal physician—Dr Alex Tan. After a short engagement, the physician could be contacted***)

[CUT/]

(***The Chinese doctor has just given an injection of penicillin to Solania. While awaiting for her to regain consciousness, the physician spares a tight prescription to Caesarea. Ljiljana does not join the two men, but is keeping an eye instead, while tending Solania***)

2). **Dialogue (C)**

Caesarea: “Doctor, how’s she?”

Dr Alex Tan: “Within my perception;
Bitter utter, she’s shock’d by th’ critical
Tormentor and the contorted tidings.”

Caesarea: “And what’s the cryptic excrescence [MT20] here?”
(***His calmness is missing***)

Dr Alex Tan: "Mister, pray! Cuddle your tenseness.
(***He claps Caesarea's shoulder reassuringly***)
Recovery and quick bones[M121] shall be placed,
In The Lord's determination, rightly,
'Tis not a bondage unto verity,
But a quirk o' natural revolution.[M122] <77)
With her anorexia and th' addition,
A symptom o' arterioclerosis and
Heart attack; flagrantly th' medical fiend,
Her perilless period may be shrunken'd
To mere the perimeter o' three weekends."

Caesarea: "Pricked alright, 'tis the unduly remark,
But lifeless's not th' final assignation,
You must at least compensate with other
Alternative of cure."

Dr Alex Tan: "In latter-day
Treatment thus far th' disease anorexia
Is measurably cureless. Apart for th' patient's
Volition excess, battles their complexity.
Likeliness if possible 'tis germane
Convenient with a traditional treatment;
Either Chinese or Malay."

Caesarea: "Hath not thou
Bound a click of reference with this score
Of generated specialists?"

Dr Alex Tan: "Yea there're.
A few of them in my encouragement.
One I'd list to introduce is a shaman—
Haji Omar. Through well information,
Many cases he hath been well-off spent."

Caesarea: "Hmm, should not it be a cost's argument,
But I bid th' uplifting treatment of her."

Dr Alex Tan: "Mister Caesarea regret thou wouldst not.
But again, wisely a repetition,
Recovery's i' God's determination,
For swinish complexity throbs the throes."

Dr Alex Tan Exits

Caesarea: "Howsoe'er sour the end taste to champ,
We have at least assuaged by the attempt."

Scene III (Same Place)

(*The poem below is for Caesarea (= Narrator), accompanying the mime action of Haji Omar*) [Music = A Scena]

'Inchoately his meditation's treat,
        Constrained complexity not his deft keel;
A shaman—religiouslier a thrill,
        Woebegone, Haji Omar is less sat'd,
That duty he speculat'd 'a thorny deal'

Ingredients of frankincense and incense,
        Is mixed up and burnt; wisp of smoke to tense,
Thoroughgoing, chanting, invoking ~ th' charm,
        Perspiration hath wett'd his shirt to warm

Heightened heed are th' lines of the Holy phrase,
        Uttered aloud; mediocrity not maze,
Moping maximal with Olan's kismet,
        Insuperable—malady still a dread

A medicinal week like cussed shortcut,
        Choiceless o' a piece of tender satisfaction,
Soured hath but each of the numbered heart,
        Her characteristic's in depletion'

3). **Dialogue**

Haji Omar: "Th' patient's spirit doesn't react unto my calling,
E'en with my usual telepathy scheme."

Caesarea: "Couldn't her redeeming feature be insisted
To react?"

Haji Omar: “The saving grace of her exaltation
Is massively lost. For it, this could mean.
Rolling clouds thus close a sparked pleasure,
R’veting association’s e’ermore a query,
Hmm! Ruthlessness th’ old, dourness th’ new,
Mere in account, mere the sundown in view.
Reward is reward or else but to mar,
Erraticly, baking hot the olden scar,
Whereby in th’ rattling heart—blood star.”(M134)

Ljiljana: “Blood star?!”<79)

Haji Omar: “A ritzy raiment calls the riches,
Squalid movement did the witches,
Grievance’s like a wall to rupture;
And the bleeding pain’s like a schist,
Scrawny phys’cality th’ nature,
Nought a remedy but all amiss.”

Ljiljana: “And the blood star
I mean?”

Haji Omar: “This operation’s considered—”

Caesarea: “Isn’t it a failure thou’rt to subjoin?”
(*Caesarea puts in his contrited voice)*

Haji Omar: “Hmm.
(*Permissibly he nods. A long pause takes over. Followingly he continues,*)

“Within ‘nother day; an apprehension,
Tho’ missing misrule, thy sister may astir,
Giving her message with explanation,
I’ possible try thyself least to obstruct,
Or dot, the later might lose in the dark,
Methink possible this’s a propinquity,
Much more towards her piece of legacy,
Adding with other major inclusions.
In propensity for a leave to leave,
Pardon me thou mayst for all the miseries.”

Caesarea: “He knows her better than me, Haji Omar.”
(***Caesarea slowly contrites***)

Haji Omar: “Mister Caesarea, pray! Don’t let thy woe
Overrules thee. It is a kismet’s flow
Which is promised.”

Scene IV (Same Place)

(***The poem below is for Choir*** (= Narrator), ***going through with the screening***)

By stages[(M125)] th’ shaman collects his items,<80)
        Fatigue’s tuning long his ashen aspect,
Far and away if uttered—grievance worms,
        Beseeming in lockjaw he is left—slack

Th' eagle, stately stamina, flies and glides,
Whining in grouch's measure, sentiment's tight,
Rigidly comprehension's Jannequin,
And Olan's despondency his demean

Futuristic gaeity ~ nay presumption,
Is within edge o' losing striking colours,
Feeling saith—prickly th' verification,
Gruelling, spasm, shiver, turn by turn spars

The five eaglets dev'lop ~ big and wiser,
As freshly as a verdant verbena,
Afirmament—guarded by their father,
When home hav' repast on a samovar

On th' airy eventide of their return;
The fourth day of the shaman's departure,
Astir Olan, guard'd by deprivation,
Tho' Aria and Ljiljana tend to assure,
But still closing speech i' laxness' seizure.

4). **Dialogue**

Ljiljana: "Lass, my dear.
(***She holds Solania's arm while the other hand gripping a bowl of chicken's soup***)
"Wherefore must split, apacely, this rel'tion?
Wherefore must not it stay? Pray lass, my dear,
Sip this flavour and livest thou unto
Thy mirth fresh."

Solania: "Auntie. (***She smiles weakly***)
"Thy voice mimic th' hue
O' my mother. Joyous I am and peaceful
At this very end."

Ljiljana: "Pray lass, if not all,
Eat this repast wilt thou? Mama's wish must
Be fulfilled."

Caesarea: "Sister Olan, thou shouldst
Not be bested by th' riling emotion,
A smudge o' lucklessness tho' worst of desperation,
Shall anon be washed by initiation."

Solania: (***takes the bowl. Silently she stares at its content. However, she returns it to Ljiljana***)
"Auntie,
I cannot. And pray pardon my discomfiture.
Piger once valued my initiation;

Every fondness in recognition,
And his aspect, existence, reverence,
Cut-and-dried my quintessential sweetie,
And his piece of candour I'm made merry,
Whilst my emotion his one gravity.
Tho' quick, still a departure and I'm lonely,
But death I'm marvell'd and free."
(***A long pause of silence between them***)
"Aria and auntie,
I thank ye both my whole life till heaven,
As a kindred of newly relation.
Diving and trimming, thus thee my Aria,
My desperation, woe, being forlorn.
Auntie, limitless love o' second mama,
Pampering my feeling that's widely torn,
Awhile in oppression and dilemma.
O! My closest kins, I've something for ye. Aria?"

Caesarea: "Sister. Thou'rt outraged for leaving th' onus,
But death's unlauded as legendary,
We, thou receivest nobly as kindred,
But, 'tis squand'ring th' utt'rance when we be left.
They, thy progenies; a wonder worths a treat,
But, 'tis squand'ring a title when theybe left—
The orphanages. Sister, pray! 'Gain said:
Must not leave us, morrow or in future.
Are we all spuriously an existence
Or valueless figures?"

Solania: (***pulls Caesarea close and cries***) O! Dear Aria.
Nay my dear, nay. Not at all i' my humor.
But I'm lost in this world with many whys,
When... my love, my passion... arrgh! "Tis pain."

Caesarea: "Sister?! Why?!"

Solania: "Aarh!"

Ljiljana: "Lass, are you alright?"

Solania: "Yea, a bit of misery; vague I'm thrown auntie."
(***She utters breathlessly but still keeps trying to smile***)
"Aria, recall thou'rt not, th' scene in the Estima?"

Caesarea: "Yea sister, I remember.
Pray, do not tense with a sputter."

Solania: "I feel the tension again and again
Striking me."
(***She pauses and rubs her chest—controlling her pain***)
"Anyway Aria, my dear,
Forget thou mustn't. Promise me?!"

Caesarea: "Sister,
Till grave I bear any promise—"

Ljiljana: "Lass, pray
Take the bit between thy teeth hereupon."

Solanla: "O! Auntie. This may my closed book.
Aria?!"

Caesarea: "I'm harkening with dispirited ears sister.
Pray! Utter something in God's name."

Solanla: "I shall but ere,
Conscientiously must be taken, a letter,
And read by thyself. And in that drawer
I have left it.
(***She points*** [as the camera takes a long shot of] ***a drawer at a corner of the bedroom***)
"Aarrgh!"
Caesarea: "Pray sister!
Read something i' God's name."
(***Urges him anxiously and starts crying***)

Solanla: (***Weakly surprised***) "Aria, thou'rt crying?
Very sweet unto my eyesight; I'm pleased.
Remember, all the statements and th' bequest
Have been compiled and signed."

Caesarea: "I know, I know.
Pray do not leave us betimes till time-worn,
Sister, read something in God's name,
O! Lord. I beg ere Thee once for all,
Do not take my sister away."

(*Solania kisses him all over his face and tightly hug Ljiljana too*)
Solanla: "Aria,
Smile for me wilt thou?"

Caesarea: "Sister?!"

Solanla: "Nay nay, pray,
The precious grin unto my Elysium."

Caesarea: (*dishearteneddly smiles and grins*)
"Sister—"

Solanla: "O! God, my Good Lord. I'm bound in glory,
All Thy gift I've used, insofar profitably,
I'm sculpting my pride for my husband,
And my magnificent brother on hand,
Also to my loving caring auntie.
Almighty God! Forgive me all past sins."

(*She silently breathes her last life; collapsing on Caesarea's embrace—a piece of lifeless rose. The rose of grandeur. Caesarea weeps. Ljiljana weeps. The scene fades* [as it shifts outdoor towards the sky])

[EFX shot of the morning sky] (*Whining on the welkin—the eagle in its utterance of great displeasure. Whilst on the rooftop, the fiv' eaglets stood stark at the eagle, and in between, blinking downward ~ at their dead mother*)

EXEUNT

Scene V (Same Place)<81)

(***It is fast to 2:00PM in the afternoon. Caesarea is*** [focused] ***reading the letter of concern, besides the title deed.*** [A figure of living Solania reads its content])

Letter: 'Aria, sister's charm sister's warmth,
The glow of Elysium smiles on me,
The glow of radiance shapes well thee,
Tho' behind th' circling nines o' solar's poll,
With all my world at fall in roll,
Ennui not ennui but ven'rat'd,
Gloomy mere; crassness' credit shar'd,
I utter nothing more of this,
For 'tis weighing elation's miss.
This my 'distinct mansion's' now thee;
The saving's accounts are all thee;
The hotel—a business of my chance,
Obvious in thy management hence.
But portions besides ***pour ta mère***,
Sister's progeny and th' needy.
Promise! Treat ne'er with negligence.
Th' fiv' emeralds for, if they're children,
Promise! A mortgage's a misuse.'

Caesarea: "Apprehend
I must my dear sister. Apprehend'd well."
(***He smiles tearfully***)

Letter: 'Aria, it is a mixed blessing,
But summoned, it worths thy venture;
My wish which's a must be brought on.
The day thereafter my quietus,
I shall not by all means buried.
A yellow gown; that's my wedding robe,
Folded neat in the pink wardrobe,
Reflecting my Halycon days;
Whilst favouritism is a hope,
Dress me, thus I'm clad i' peace's rhythm,
Whilst within fairness in spectrum,
Within thine effort but much not,
Or a tsarina's pose utmost wott'd.
Lay the corse at the veranda,
When midnight's on night's sierra,
Yell up th' firmament ~ a signal;
"'***Thy truelove's here in revered sleep,***
Bring her with thee in heaven's trip,
As majesty as thy love's keep.'"

Caesarea: "I will my dearest sister."

Letter: "Aria, with this's th' ultimatum,
As glowing as the love 'tween us,
I am wanting thine agreement,
To meet all these to fulfilment.
And this thy place ~ as home from home,
With kisses from me that ne'er last,
As well as thee—adieu, my dear.'

[CUT/]

[The camera pans as] (***Caesarea busying himself to accomplish the request. Swiftly with care, he executes the work with the help of Ljiljana. The body of Solania, thereafter a ceremonial bath, is then clothed with the yellow gown***)

[CUT/]

(***Eventide calls. The preparation is almost completed. The corpse is made as fine; in which beseems that Solania is still sleeping***)

[CUT/]

(***The wall clock is nearing ten minutes to twelve midnight*** [as viewed by the camera in a medium range shot. Shifting, the camera then pans] ***Caesarea, whom is anxiously sweating, carries the corpse to the veranda.*** [Taking away the focusing position, the camera now gives a close shot of] ***Ljiljana sits and watches from a distance***)

[CUT/]

(***He is*** [seen] ***laying the corpse on a long bench. Admiring it for a moment***)

[CUT/]

(***12:00 midnight. The wind is gushing; stirring to a windy atmosphere but without the arrival of rain nor thunder. Caesarea looks up at the firmament, temporising***)

5). **Monologue** (*Aria Parlante with music for Caesarea*)
(***He wails the verses with daring loudness***)

Caesarea: "Night's arriving, wind is calling,
Speak myself in delirium's ting,
Demist'd my humor with dolour,
This demise I'm not asking for,
I'm enough with all these grievanc's,
Chilling my warmness, dependence;
For th' love I've wanted but hath lost

Jannequin! Th' eagle o' dominion,
Comest thou! With veneration,
Uxorious as th' olden utt'rance,
I'm valiant for this valediction,
But this loss I wouldn't pardon,
Jannequin! Th' eagle o' dominion,
Comest thou now! With hearty zip,
'Thy truelove's here in revered sleep,
Bring her with thee in heaven's trip,
As majesty as thy love's keep.'"

(***The wind gushes ~ heavily than before.*** [A long shot] ***One of the small flower's vasts falls and crashes.*** [Shifting to another scene] ***One of the tamarind grove's branches, snatches, with a long cracking sound***)

[CUT/]

[EFX effect] (***A white figure comes from a distance—whining. Caesarea waits in silence. The preoccupation of the arrival puts Caesarea's and Ljiljana's builds to palpitate. The eagle, as it reaches closer to the veranda, in out of its ordinary, has come in extrasize form.***

Certain and sharp, it watches Caesarea while alighting on Solania's chest. Caesarea stands speechless for a moment. The eagle stretches its claws on the gown and followingly deepens them into it. Brushing its beak on Solania's lips—it squawks twice)

Caesarea: "Jannequin! The living of enterprise,
Insufficient with sorry for this d'mise,
Merely nought I could hav' ventured to save,
But He knows my woe; tho' insult'd as naïve,
This experience is my unrelieved gloom.
Jannequin, the grandeur look that could loom,
Tho' sister Olan hath eternally gone,
Thou must save the course; thy return my vaunt,
By and by meeting us and thy children;
I'm here standing a dutiful guardian,
Whom shall father them; heed with love—heightened,
'Till their exaltation beseems i' heaven."

(*The fowl cries once like it is comprehensible. Skyward it takes its wing, while carrying Solania like a haycock. Both her hands drooping aside. Caesarea takes his last kiss on her fingers 'till the corpse reaches out from his touch. The whine echoes all the way until to its disappearance*)

[CUT/]

(*Caesarea and Ljiljana stand behind the veranda's railing in a melancholia. Both of them wave to the valediction*)

Caesarea: Adieu sister Olan. May God bless thee t' heaven."

A Better Life After Tomorrow <81a) (S.xv)

(iFAN Music & Art W.002)

Sung Verses (Song) [*Free Verse for Caesarea* (Singer) *and Ljiljana* (Singing Echo)]

Proseable Verse

After the sun
Sunk in the west,
You will anon fade
By the change of time

All th' sweet memories
Would then be shadows,
And may not be 'live
Again, as before...

Chorus

Although my mind
Is still here thinkin',
Waving the time
To come back again

But it's still the same
As before,
This story this hist'ry,
Will begone—forever

Bridge

When I write
I hymn it a piece of music,
Hoping in sorrow
For a better life ~
After tomorrow

▬ ▬ ▬

(***The song's outro leads the scene to its fadeout***)

EXEUNT

Scene VI (Same Place)(82)

(***Still the same night. The wind has calmed to an airy night***)

[CUT/]

(***Caesarea and Ljiljana have been abed. But Caesarea, has kept shedding tears even after fallen asleep. The roundly dejection has pressurised his emotion—overly***)

[CUT/]

[A close shot of] (***The oversized parrot's cage has now transformed into an aviary. Two of the fiv' eaglets are sleepless. Blinking their eyes repeatedly. All of a sudden… their feathers detach. In a blurred moment, they have all transformed into five youngsters.***

Overlying amongst themselves—in the pokey place. The two sisters, Solace The Compass and Lovepress The West, are unabed; but, they are discussing among each other)

6). **Dialogue** (or Singing in Prose)

Lovepress The West: "You seem older than me. You know my name, you brown eyes?"

Solace The Compass: "I don't know you. But, you know mine, you blue eyes?"

Lovepress The West: "A regret for you, no."

Solace The Compass: "Fiddlestick is dull. And dull, daft and bolshy are our joy."

(*They pause the melodic conversation for a short while*)

Lovepress The West: "I think we're sisters and brothers plus these dummies. Sickening weightiness aren't they?"

(*Solace The Compass has beseemed not listening but changes her view, nonetheless*)

Solace The Compass: "Can't you see the clothes over there?"

Lovepress The West: "Yes. Then what?"

Solace The Compass: "Shut your wide mouth, will you? The people upstairs are sleeping."

Lovepress The West: "Methink they're just deaf like these dummies. Eh? You look like older than me, don't you?"

Solace The Compass: "Perhaps. These fellers upstairs mightn't be like us."

Lovepress The West: "In what sense?"

Solace The Compass: "We're all naked. It makes me self-shame."

Lovepress The West: "Er! I don't care their opinions. Yesterday—we're flying creatures don't we?"

Solace The Compass: "Yes. But 'tis not anymore now."

Lovepress The West: "But I'm in my felicity to whatever state. Don'twe've father and mother?"

Solace The Compass: "I don't know. Perhaps if likely, they're ours."

Lovepress The West: "Why they put us in this cage?"

Solace The Compass: "Don't stretch your wide gob further. Go get some sleep."

Lovepress The West: "Hmm!" (*She wimpers irritably,*) "You're bad to me."

Solace The Compass:(*hardly stretches her hand, she fondles Lovepress' hair while placating,*) "Alright, alright. I'm sorry, I know I'm bad."

Lovepress The West: "Hmm! You're bad."

Solace The Compass: "Alright, I'm bad. Just go and get some sleep, can't you?"

Lovepress The West: "Hmm! Bad."

(*Throwing water on the midnight fire—Lovepress has gone asleep. Leaving Solace with eyes blinking; studying the surroundings*)

EXEUNT

Scene VII (Same Place)

(*The morn is cherishing weariness.* [The camera pans as] *Ljiljana keeps her routine duty at the kitchen—preparing breakfast. But the incongruity of Solania's death has tinged her temperament; aslant to shed tears*)

[CUT/]

[An above shot as] (***Caesarea lingers to the hall, with wetted hair after bath. Howsoever, giddiness has partly controlled his walking. Standing for a brief moment, he bleakly watches Solania's portrait. Thereafter, he proceeds to the porch***)

[CUT/]

[Zoom] (***The fiv' children are still sleeping***)

[CUT/]

(***Caesarea opens the entrance door. His astonishment alit the moment he bumps into the children. Apacely he unlocks the avery***)

7). **Dialogue**

Caesarea: "I'm shoved to disbelief my Gracious Lord.
(***He wakes the children up; effecting a fatherly care***)
"My sweet little children, ascending me
Into seven heaven. A mystique! Wake up!
(***The three boys shake their heads as they are helped exiting the crowded avery by Caesarea. Solace sleepily follows while Lovepress is shouldered by him***)
"Children, I'm nowise liking to place ye all here.
Come inside."

Solace The Compass: "Aren't you our—"
(***Queries her while clutching Caesarea's arm***)

Caesarea: (***says while kissing her forehead,***)
"Father! Your dad
My little princess. Pray all! Come inside."

Amethyst The East: "Dad,
(***He queries and nudges,***) "Why are we naked and dirty?"

Caesarea: "For God is partial to love ye all more.
(***He calls Ljiljana***)
Mama! Come over here. We've got something at present."

[CUT/]

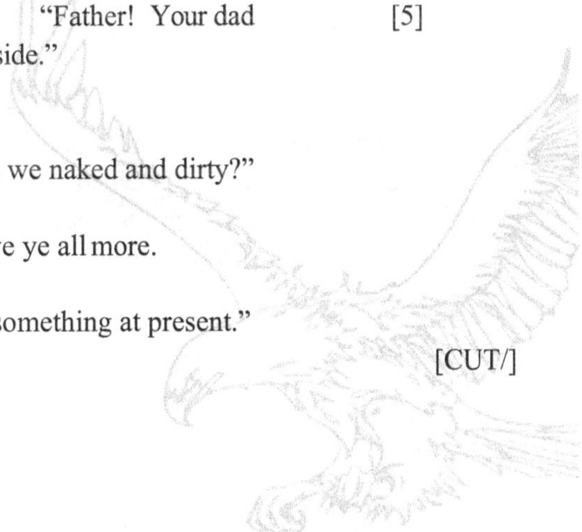

(*Ljiljana strides into the hall. She intends to smile, but, stuck in won- derment—instead*)

Ljiljana: "O! Heavens above! How pretty they are.
What have we got here?!"
(*Ljiljana embraces each of them; one by one ~ with a kiss*)

Solace The Compass: "May I know her, dad?"

Caesarea: "Of course thou mayst. She is thy grandma."

Ljiljana: "Sweeties, I am spotlighting the high spot,
O' my discoveries with ye all."

Solace The Compass: (*puts in apacely*) "Grandma, your eyes are red."

Ljiljana: "Sweetie, red is tears, whereby tears is joy."

(*Aside — in mixed voices, Lovepress softly snivels as she awakes on Caesarea's shoulder*)
Lovepress The West: "I'm still bad."

(*Aside — in mixed voices, Caesarea coaxes Lovepress while fondling her hair*)
Caesarea: "O! Dear. You're not bad. For luck
Is engrossing in you."

Lovepress The West: "Hmm father. When as a bird, I'm hungry. Would I be same as that, now?"

Caesarea: "Sure you may not. I'll assure you well-fed
All the time. Before that, give dad, your first sweet kiss."
(*Lovepress kisses him on the cheek. Proudly he replies,*)
Hmm, that is what I've ever desired."

Ljiljana: "Alright everybody." (***Commandingly she calls***) "The English breakfast is growing cold. I'll bath all of you before that. Aria! Look, search, and pick any small dress for all these children."

Caesarea: "As thou saith."

Antidoubt The South: (***Aside – in mixed voices***) "Grandma, the water is cold. We are freezing."

Amethyst and Nixloath: "Yea! He is correct."

Ljiljana: "There's warm water for ye all. But let me tell ye something. The germs, the itching worms, might hunt ye if thy builds have an improper wash."

Amethyst, Nixloath & Antidoubt: "Eee! Ooh! Noo."

Solace & Lovepress: "Hmm! Bad!"

(***All of them run into the bathroom, accompanied by Ljiljana—busted a gut. Meanwhile, before forwarding upstairs, Caesarea stares at Solania's portrait and utters***)

Caesarea: Sister, 'tis betwixt mirth and dreariness,
Getting through a loss and a find in spurts,
My stability's vitiat'd; bowed spirit,
If, if I have most my vest'd interest,
I shall formulate unto thy rebirth,
Sharing full with thee this mystical verve.
My sister, if thou couldst hold them now,
Patent passion; thou wouldst not pause to paw,
Howsoever, though thee fast heaven-high,
Thy spirit e'er besides me in particular
For th' tender touch on thy belov'd children."
(***He leaves*** [off-screen], ***giving away to his moodiness***)

EXEUNT

Scene VIII (Same Place)

The family are having their leisure pursuit. Lovepress is nestling in Ljiljana's embrace.

[Close shot] (***A pop selection in low volume from the cassette deck is taken pleasure by Nixloath and Antidoubt, surroundingly***)

[Shifting to pan] (***Amethyst, whom has just taken his swim, is helping Caesarea and Solace, carrying two trays of light repast with a box containing the five emeralds to the hall***)

[CUT/]

(***A pause of relaxation, while Caesarea and Ljiljana are attending the children's mannerism. Opening the conversation, Caesarea asks Amethyst; of whom is leaning relaxingly besides him on the sofa***)

8). **Dialogue**

Caesarea: "Dear, do you like 'nother drinks o' this syrup?"

Amethyst The East: "Umm no." (***Shaking his head, he elongates,***) "Dad, what's that?"
(***He points at the box of which is still unopen on the tray***)

Solace The Compass: "Yes dad. What is that actually?"
(***Impatiently she adds***)

Caesarea: (***looks at Ljiljana doubtfully***) "Mama?!"

Ljiljana: (***apprehendedly nods***) "Yea!"

Caesarea: "My children."
(***Signalling them with paternal tenderness***)
"Come close to me."

Antidoubt & Nixloath: "Dad, that thing gives us great sound."

Caesarea: "Dear, thou callest it—music.
'Tis composed i' several genres
To please our hearing, conceptually.
Haply, befriend our loneliness;
If not ayely but certain times."

Antidoubt & Nixloath: "What type of music, the last we've heard, a moment ago?"

Caesarea: "'Tis a ballad rock of western culture."

Antidoubt The South: "That's great."

Caesarea: "Alright."
(***He reanimates the previous topic. Opening the box, he takes out one of the emeralds; which is set in a gold necklace***)
"Children—"

Nixloath The North: "Wow! It is wonderful, dad."

Amethyst The East: "You, shut your mouth. Let father does the talking."

Caesarea: "Never mind son. It doesn't matter.
Fortunately they are wonderful, dear.
These charmingly gifts here are all for ye,
Each o' its wearer o' these necklaces shall be
Named simultaneously."

Lovepress The West: "Yea dad. I want a name for myself."

Amethyst The East: "Me too!"

Solace, Nixloath & Antidoubt: "We too!"

Caesarea: "Good. Alright. The elder shall get the present first."

Solace The Compass: (*interpolates*) "Dad, I'm the eldest."

Caesarea: "Come, you brown eyes. Give me a kiss first.
(*Solace kisses Caesarea*)
"Alright. This's yours—Solace The Compass."
(*Caesarea wreathes Solace with the necklace*)

Amethyst The East: "I'm the second, dad."

Caesarea: "Come, you brown eyes boy."
(*Amethyst kisses Caesarea on the cheek and Caesarea returns it lovingly*)
"Son, this's yours—Amethyst The East.
And be a brave man i' your future."

Amethyst The East: "Yes dad. I shall fulfill your ambition."

Nixloath The North: "I'm the third, dad." (*Says him in a chuckle*)

Caesarea: "Oh you! Whom shall be the crimson crooner.
Come here.
(*Caesarea kisses and tickles the child*)
"This is yours crooner—Nixloath The North.
Son, be a generous man in thy future."

Nixloath The North: "Alright dad. I'm going to that."

Lovepress The West: "I'm the fourth, dad."

Antidoubt The South: "No dad! She's the fifth. I'm the fourth."

Lovepress The West: "You're bad. I'm the fourth, you the thumping gaffer with tidemark. Dad?!"

Antidoubt The South: "This could sound better to your whimpering habit, runt." (*Antidoubt gives Lovepress a whimsy yet annoying smile*)

Lovepress The West: "Dad?! (*She snivels*)

(*Ljiljana, Caesarea and Solace laugh to the scenario. While aside, Amethyst pushes Antidoubt; a reminder not to lengthen the disturbance*)

Caesarea: "No.. no.. alright. No quarrel. Lady's first. Come."

Lovepress The West: "Thanks dad."
(*Lovepress comes closer and embraces Caesarea. A fly of kiss is given to her by him*)

Caesarea: "Make sure you don't lose it, okay?"

Lovepress The West: "Sure dad."

Caesarea: "Good. This is yours—Lovepress The West."

Antidoubt The South: "And me, dad?"
(*Caesarea uplifts Antidoubt, and puts the cheeky boy on his laps. And folds Antidoubt in his arms*)

Caesarea: "Thou mustn't be a fop merely just, but,
But also a lettered man, son. This yours—
Antidoubt The South."

Antidoubt The South: "I shall be a great man, dad."

Caesarea: "Right! Into my fabulous hearing."

Lovepress The West: "Dad, where's mom?"

(***Caesarea watches Solania's portrait, and then Ljiljana ~ seeking answers. Hardly he puts,***)

Caesarea: "My dear children; mother's choice is heaven,
But she hath begone for a long voyage,
Plausibly, she might or might not return,
But her love, hereditary are left much
For us all; certainty not in languor,
And every of her passion premier—
The very keen of her demands entire—
Merely our transported heart of joy.
Though she stays afar; a sight is e'er trapped,
But her entrench'd spirit is within ye,
And th' mother's love is here part of me.
But this love could be felt i' equalizer,
Merely with thy smile and laughter."

Lovepress: "I love you, dad."

Solace, Amethyst, Nixloath & Antidoubt: "We all do love you, dad, and grandma."

EXEUNT

ACT V

Scene I (In the British Airways Jumbo Jet Aircraft)

Sitting in a business suite, the grown-up Lovepress is smiling comfortably alone, while looking outside the window. A middle-age traveller, sitting beside, starts to put a query.

1). **Dialogue**

Traveller: "The landau is an artefact—a transport,
But the latter-day's limousine in draw,
Blithely lady, may this not overwrought,
What is the time, now; accuracy pure[(M129)]?"

Lovepress The West: "Irr'pressibly[(M130)] thy query for me,$_{<84)}$
Mid-century extrovert like father,
Whose numinously mien my express glee,
'Tis six even—handicap flat rather."

Traveller: "I'm a trifle flummox'd with an ill watch,[(M131)]
When a foolhardlier hath act'd a fluster,
A daughter a child once wanted at notch,
But sons, a generosity; little gauche,
Worthy lady, my child. Art thou a scholar?"

Lovepress The West: "The alternation of world's towering,
Of staggeringly movement an inkling,
An M.S.[(M132)]-literate o' Stamford this year,
An opthalmology nurtured; oculist l'ter."

Traveller: "In pondered heart, loveable and weighty—
The father; a stamina to thy glory,
If rank toleration thou art in tow,
What's thee kin call'd; if I could wot to stow?"

Lovepress The West: "Aye, candidly. Thou'rt ingenious in there,
My father—a symbol; a magnificence's air,
As sibling similar a compass; a jest,
An infusion—I am Lovepress The West."

Traveller: "A wallflower; peace is an insist'd aim,
In perception, best; complexion at rest,
Thy name's glamorising unto thy fame
To thine intend'd—his fortunate empress."

Lovepress The West: "Thank you."

(***She beholds outside the window, waving to two eagles of passerby.*** [An EFX long shot of] ***The eagles fly close to the aircraft before diving below and leave***)

Traveller: "To whom art thou giving thy wave?"

Lovepress The West: "My two wing'd brothers."

Traveller: "Those eagles without thou'th meant?"

Lovepress The West: "Why? Is it surprising?"

Traveller: "For Godsake I'm,
Trippingly alied log!" (***He faints***)

Lovepress The West: "Ah! Sorry sir." (***She chuckles***)

EXEUNT
[CUT/]

(*The aircraft is close to make a landing at the Kuala Lumpur International Airport, Sepang*)

[CUT/]

[A long shot] (*A Proton Saga cab leaves the waiting hall towards the city centre*)

Scene II (Yow Chuan Plaza's Square, Ampang)

[EFX shot] (*The two eagles glide downwards to a car park. Signalling themselves into a momentary separation. While one alights on a red volkswagen, the other beside a heap of social refuse.*

Transforming themselves, into Antidoubt and Nixloath; in their early twenties. Clad in leather wear—trousers, jackets and boots, they have fast appeared 'classic rockers')

2). **Dialogue**

Antidoubt The South: "Methink if limp, our inordinate length o' venture,
Tho' ne'er insatiable but del'berate.
Fortunately we haven't squirt'd by pressure,
For th' turboprop point'd us unexceptional;
A guesstimate's worst than fossilisation.
But a forte, Amy's love fort'fies my luck."

Nixloath The North: “Swiftly soluble unto the affair.
Haven’t thou playest not th’ fatuous Graces?[M133]
Communing for kin’s bond should top thy brain,
‘Tis a suspended yearning for Lovepress.
How many years there’re? Meet for three seasons,
Wouldst thou melt into this desire?”

Antidoubt The South: “A melodramatic creature, wouldn’t she?
Just I don’t mind our discordant tumour,[85][M134]
For the olden reminiscence’s a tumble.[M135]
But not father, Solace; swelling liking,[M136]
And grandma, sweetening my huffish sting,
I’m a stoic[M137] whene’er I treat ‘em in prayer.”

Nixloath The North: “They’re placed in us; above hunch—Heavens.
Heartwarmingly, thou shouldst show to her,
For replacing th’ lost things which staple thee aye—
Heavyheartedly. Wouldn’t ‘t be i’ mem’rial?”

Antidoubt The South: “Hard by my hankering,[M138] where’s mother’s grave?
I’d frame a circuit[M139] to recall our history,
Am I fooled by reservation or what?
Credibly I am subresolute for
Chumming Lovepress up.”

Nixloath The North: “I am purposeful for
Such principals. And the hesitancy
Drives th’ time hectic for thou’rt heeding to pick
Up Amy, while me, slog for my Tiara;
And, thou’rt confined—”

Antidoubt The South: “In thy category?”[(M140)][<86)]

Nixloath The North: “Rideless o’ two wheels.”

Antidoubt The South: “We request privacy.”

Nixloath The North: “Y’art choiceless to-night.”

Antidoubt The South: “I shall moderate,
There’s nay stringent reason.”

Nixloath The North: “Supportable
With a bet?’

Antidoubt The South: “I shall plan with that eagle,
Usual, cool of strangeness, someday.”

[EFX shot] (***Antidoubt points at a bald eagle*** (Jannequin’s formation)***; flying atop them, southwards***)

Nixloath The North: “Dastardly thee.
I am dauntless for a confrontation,
Haven’t decide to know why?”

Antidoubt The South: “I shouldn’t
Be prostrate with a warrant.”

Nixloath The North: (***slaps Antidoubt’s shoulder***) “So, wanting
A promotion for a release? Thou’rt going
To the wall with the idea. Wagging first
Pulse of debt—the publicity.”[(M141)]

Antidoubt The South: “Naught thus
In utterance.” (***While watching the pedestrians about***)

Nixloath The North: "Alright. But recking fast,
And absolutely, ere absenting for
Thy wench's fair. Shouldst it be remark'd or
Just a note? Th' stat'd fowl ere fatherly attend'd,
Still a comrade; and haply, a blood relation.
Therefore play ne'er with him, nor anytime;
Or shall count th' cost at thy favourite's prime. <87)
(*They enter the plaza.* [In a long shot] *Amy is ambling like a catwalk model towards them. Before leaving, Nixloath finalizes,*)
"Though she's enchanting, but subject'd second
As a privilege; the eagle is the main."

Nixloath Exits

Antidoubt The South: "I assume both hot subjects."

Amy: "Hi Nix! Ant!
Where is Nixloath going Ant?"
(*She watches Nixloath leaving in speechless manner*)

Antidoubt The South: "Taking his brand'd
Car and leave us back on th' easy bike; my trend,
To Lovepress party."

Amy: "Ant, darling. He's thy brother anyway."

Antidoubt The South: "Thine odour shifts my knifed primness away.
Er! Few packaged surprises. For whom're they?"

Amy: "Lovepress, thy father, grandma."

Antidoubt The South: "How 'bout me?"

Amy: "There're two but betimes this moment."

Antidoubt The South: "Wherefore?"

Amy: "'Tis climbing fast to be taken up for the ride,
Whereat this's not yet our meeting's tail end,
So, when the moment's in its mellowness,(M144)
Thou shalt befriend the gold favour."<88) (M144)

Antidoubt The South: "Really?
I love thee." (***He kisses her***)

[CUT/]

[The camera swivels as] (***Amy and Antidoubt rides on their Harley Roadster. The scene fades as the easy riders leave the place***)

EXEUNT

Scene III (Concorde Hotel, Kuala Lumpur)

In the lobby, Amethyst in his late twenties, wearing lounge suit; is making his way to the restaurant.

[Mixed screen] (***One round dinner table for fourteen diners, has set the whole family. Caesarea is casted a mid-fifties father, Ljiljana as an old grandmother, Nixloath, Antidoubt and his fiancée Amy, meanwhile Solace in her early thirties is sitting beside Caesarea, in a concerned conversation. A restaurant supervisor, Lee, is serving them with drinks***)

3). **Dialogue**

Caesarea: "Solace."

Solace The Compass: "Yea father. Thou lookest borthered."

Caesarea: (*emphasises Lovepress' absence throughout*)
"Sit, cheerless is cold; stand, tremor a mole,
I'm modish to my perennial muddle,[M145]
Should Lovepress be guided by a chaperon
To this dinner?"

Solace The Compass: "Father, agrieve must not,
Lest perchance, she hath a fused timepiece— [M146] <89)
Frustrating her functions or a blockage
With uncertain peak o' traffic alignment.
Father—an hour in addition, pray?"

Caesarea: "A bloomer this unblitheness methink a fusspot.
Isn't mine convoluted to the core?
I shouldn't gesture for mere fussiness,
What a simultaneous silken exhibition;
Arrival, unasked. Amy, is it you?"

Amy: (*approaches Caesarea and kisses him*)
"I'm, father. Tho' this a parcel by a whisker,[M147]
But a nightlight's delight—a jocose brush,[M148]
For thee and grandma."

Caesarea: "What a nice surprise.
Thank you.
(*While watching Amy's direction towards Ljiljana, he addresses Antidoubt*)
"Ant, thy maiden is much a gaily
Gardenia."

Antidoubt The South: "Dad, nay gainsaying of my
Spelt gladness. Damn pretty isn't she?"

Caesarea: "Hm.
Could wind thee down in fay's sward."

Nixloath The North: (*aside adds*) "Addendum
That he should revolves around her flawless."

Solace The Compass: (*to Antidoubt*)
"Must be evermore in thine heart's content."

Antidoubt The South: "I shall be untactless in my leisure."

Amy: (***frolicsomely puts,***) "He's my lyrical Martian."
(***They are all driven to laughter***)

Ljiljana: (*inserts*) "Anon sure,
Binding thine hearts amongst thyselves, my dear."

Caesarea: "I' my intercession, 'tshall be intriguing
Relation under the olive branch."

Amethyst The East: (aside—***in mixed voices, he simpers***)
"Lee, ev'ning. Haven't taken your dinner?"

Lee: (aside—***in mixed voices***)
"Mister Amethyst, sure, sure I hav' sir,
Anyway, the buffet dinner's ready,
But father figure's wish's favoured primly
With pre-serve in light repasts of which are
Butterscotch sundae, cakes and lemon tea."

Amethyst The East: (aside—***in mixed voices***)
"Anything that he desires special.
(***Diverts his attention towards Lorraine, the waiter's captain, Amethyst accosts***)
"Lorraine. Taking overtime?"

Lorraine: "I'm on night shift, sir."

Amethyst The East: "How's your child, Smartie? Does he gets better
After the treatment?"

Lorraine: "Gladly nowadays
He is on an even keel. Speak no ace
Notably, I'm indebt'd with thy kindness."

Amethyst The East: "Put it aside, there's naught much from me,
Besides, noteworthy, I should announce 't here."

Lorraine: "Aye, sir."

Amethyst The East: "Naught momentuous but there will be
An increment in your oft-salary,
In effect this coming moon."

Lorraine: "Er! How glad I am."

Amethyst The East: "Thou'rt pitched for bone. Pinch th' pity and work some
For thyself. Suggest th' valu'd but norm'd viands
In thine angle as possible; no defiance,
Upstairs, I've got a few for thee. Eat it,
Eat better, okay?"

Lorraine: "Aye my thankful wit."

(***Passes Mohan, the restaurant manager, handling two bowls of mushroom soup***)

Mohan: (***addresses Amethyst***) "Thou art having the state of thy father,
A sociable custodian and gen'rous."

Amethyst The East: "Ah! A stand—not to that particular."

Mohan: "But the colour's getting into a glow."
(***Arranging the dishes on the table, he changes his attention towards Caesarea***)
"Sir, pray! Hav' this as an opening taste,
A speciality from the chef."

Caesarea: "Mohan!
As such of old I'm losing th' attendance,
Whereto world thou hath lost?"

Mohan: "Five thorough moons
Honeymoon with my belov'd lady."

Caesarea: "Where?"

Mohan: "Pyramids o' Giza."

Caesarea: "Patent banter, eh?"(M150)
(***Tickling Mohan's waist***)<91)

Mohan: "Ouch!
(*He giggles*) "That chatterbox darling hath request'd
For Smaland, but, we've occasionally
End'd at th' Harvey Bay, Australia."

Caesarea: "Really?!"

Mohan: "Miraculously all round with the whales."

Caesarea: "Azany wouldn't they?"

Mohan: "One golden hole
To the goal."

(***Amethyst nears Caesarea, take his hand and kisses it with habitual merit***)

Amethyst The East: "Dad, grandma, delight'd be y'all
With th' decent menu, and pardon me yet
For attending ye tardily."

Ljiljana: "Dear sweet,
Intermission couples might. Thy duty
Decisively, esteemed in my apprehension."
(***Amethyst stands hard by Ljiljana and exchanges kisses with her***)

Caesarea: "Amethyst?"

Amethyst The East: "Aye, dad."

Caesarea: "When, yet untimely,
Th' turn to erase thy bachelor's profile?"

Amethyst The East: "Recurrent nay, father. Recalcitrant
I am quite for a flirtation. For thine
Example, I'm at ease to immitate."

(*Within, Lovepress hastily enters with her swinging handbag. She kisses and embraces Ljiljana apacely*)

Lovepress The West: (aside—*in mixed voices*)
"Grandma, glows my gladness to meet you 'gain."

Ljiljana: (aside—*in mixed voices*)
"O! Dear, signifying my fullblown mirth above
With thine emergence. Why short of luggage?"

Lovepress The West: "I have left them at Amethyst's office."

(*Caesarea catches Lovepress in his eyes and he strikes with a high voice—pretending serious*)

Caesarea: "Lovepress?! Going to Mars art thou not?"

Lovepress The West: (*approaches Caesarea*) "O! Dad, [80]
My tardiness I am in tears for it,
Not up for Mars; mere with love, choice, passion,
But solely for thee."

(*Lovepress and Caesarea hug together*)

Caesarea: "Enrapturing my
Thankfulness to Heaven." [84]

(*The others, in a clap amidst expanded laughter. Meanwhile, Amethyst assisting another two waiters, serving the complete dinner. Whereas Mohan, Lee, Lorraine and Chef Lombardo re-enter with additional dishes while hymning their choral tunes*)

New Joy, No Poignancy,
New World for Everybody <93 (S.xvi)

Sung Verses (*Aria di mezzo carattere*)

Intro Refrain: (Mohan, Lee, Lorraine & Chef Lombardo)

New joy, no poignancy,
New world for everybody (2X)

Mohan's Verse

Doing justice unto harmony,
And there's a main in staunch kinship, (XII 52)
Once time act'd but a lethargy,
Hence oscillates a scenic manuscript

An action of praised deed
Demolish's dejection,
A long term delectation,
Demerits not a heed,
Deliberation's fine,
Glory's treasure a find

Th' olden worth o' Jannequin,
Was willed to Solania,
When once told, tears in screen;
Begon'd hath th' modest queen,
Sine die but Caesarea

Staff: "Mayst thou live in fortune all the time, sir!"

Th' Flv' Children: "Our beloved father, our legend."

Caesarea: "I'm momentously proud with ye all."

Chef Lombardo's & Lee's Verses <94)

From Grand Baie 'till here,
I've been sat'd[M153] for twelve years,
Workmates, the owner—my dear,
All have attained their spurs[M154]

A great toast in the morn,
Designer speciality at dinner,
Finest guild hath reborn,
These, tonic gifts of masterful booster
(***A brief laughter from all***)

One mooncake is shared by all,
Congeniality wins nay brawl,
Nought tends for a breakage,
Anon but o' winning edge

All stick'd a boon companion,
With motions o' a gild'd pigeon,
I'm localis'd, we're localis'd
Under this one roof—princely priced

Caesarea: "On a label of luck, forasmuch as we're all in."
(*laughingly*)

Refrain: (The hotel's staff and the family)
New joy, no poignancy,
New world for everybody (2X)

Lorraine's and the other three waiters' verses
A flying horse in spring,
A mystique on the brink;
Its chitter-chattered wonder
Is hence everlasting,
E'ery inch unto this laughter
Hath its gracious vim in quiver

A situation's assum'd th' finest
When mishap's parting from us,
While outbrave any resistance,
Our mirth is now not in askance

Refrain: (The hotel's staff and the family)
New joy, no poignancy,
New world for everybody (2X)

The moment of the finale has drawn the whole family to dine their dinner; kicking their heels to the saviour taste. The rollicking time, thereafter, bridges them unto the moonlit night.

[Mixed screen; EFX close shot] (***The eagle alights on the bungalow's rooftop; resting there while praising the still full moon***)

THE END

Typewritten piece completed: 10:45AM – 27th July 1998
Retyped masterpiece and edited: 04:07PM – 05th December 2021

(W.104 of Ido Firadyanié Art Nouveau Collections)

Glossary

Eagle and th' Fiv' Eggs

(5 Acts Comically Operatic Play/Film)
(W.104 of Ido Firadyanié Art Nouveau Collections)

1). The Songs in Eagle and th' Fiv' Eggs

[PART I]

S.i)	To Thy Best	(pg.17) (<1) 1	(I.i.73-100)
S.ii)	Aria di Portamento	(pg.20) (<5)	(I.ii.26-45)
S.iii)	I'm A Wage Slave	(pg.23) (<8)	(I.iii.1-22)
S.iv)	"Sure I Will, My Dear Sister"	(pg.29) (<12)	(I.iii.108-132)
S.v)	"Here I'm but on the Cloud"	(pg.39) (<19a)	(II.ia.35-65)
S.vi)	The Appetizing Viands	(pg.43) (<22)	(II.ib.93-111)
S.vii)	If Perchance	(pg.59) (<31a)	(II.iiia.37-51)
S.viii)	A Sonnet (Cavatina)	(pg.64) (<33)	(II.iv.52-65)
S.ix)	"Revelation of the Heart"	(pg.94) (<54)	(III.iv.53-88)
S.x)	Honey (Prose)	(pg.108) (<61a)	(III.vi.19-40)
S.xi)	A Cavatina	(pg.112) (<62a)	(III.vi.91-134)
S.xii)	'Thy Love' (Prose)	(pg.115) (<63a)	(III.vi.135-160)

[PART II]

S.xiii)	"Captive Don't by Deploration"	(pg.120) (<64)	(IV.i.16-67)
S.xiv)	'Posthaste Postie'	(pg.132) (<74a)	(IV.iia.81-104)
S.xv)	A Better Life After Tomorrow(Prose)	(pg.155) (<81a)	(IV.v.107-127)
S.xvi)	New Joy, No Poignancy, New World for Everybody	(pg.181) (<94)	(V.iii.85-135)

Glossary

Eagle and th' Fiv' Eggs

(5 Acts Comically Operatic Play/Film)
(W.104 of Ido Firadyanié Art Nouveau Collections)

2). Translation of French Verses & Proses

F.i) (II.ia.1-2) ***Mere, je suis rentré!*** = Mother, I've returned home!
Une surprise d'après midi. = An afternoon's surprise. (<18) (pg.37)

F.ii) (II.ia.20) ***Un on-dit pas, vraiment.*** = A rumour not, really. (<19) (pg.38)

F.iii) (II.ia.23) ***Celui-ci!*** = This one! or This! (<19) (pg.38)

F.iv) (II.ia.34) ***D'accord! Je il ferai maintenant.*** = Alright! I will do it now. (<19a) (pg.39)

F.v) (II.ib.68) ***Mere, qu'est-ce que c'est?*** = Mother, what is it? (<21) (pg.42)

F.vi) (II.iiia.27) ***Mere, je connais.*** = Mother, I know or I understand. (<31) (pg.58)

F.vii) (III.i.30-31) ***Merci! Madame.*** = Thank you! Madam. (<35a) (pg.67)

F.viii) (III.i.32) ***Ne vous en faites pas.*** = Never mind or It is a small matter. (<35a) (pg.67)

F.ix) (III.i.36) ***Monsieur, attendre!*** = Gentleman, wait! (<35a) (pg.67)

F.x) (III.i.42) ***Je suis une autochtone de Lyon,*** = I'm a native of Lyon or I'm from Lyon. (<36a) (pg.68)

F.xi) (III.i.45) ***Sans maintenant; pas pertinence,*** (here ***sans = sans- gêne***) = Thoughtlessness, now; nay relevance (Meaning that: It is only to be a relic) (<36a) (pg.68)

F.xii) (III.iv.10-12) ***Le diner est délicieux, mon Olan,***
Qui convient à par acquit de conscience;
Ne plus savoir que faire le mien.
= Th' dinner's delicious my Olan,
Suitably for peace o' mind,
At end of wit of mine. (<52) (pg.92)

F.xiii) (III.iv.89) ***Ma chérie*** = My darling. (<55a) (pg.96)

F.xiv) (III.iv.89) ***Oui*** = Yes (other lines too) (<55a) (pg.96)

F.xv) (IV.i.79) ***je ne sais quoi*** = a quality that cannot be described easily. (<68) (pg.124)

Glossary

Eagle and th' Fiv' Eggs

(5 Acts Comically Operatic Play/Film)
(W.104 of Ido Firadyanié Art Nouveau Collections)

3). Words, sentences, and meanings

ACT I

M1) (I.i.par.14) pallet – is used as verb from noun (<1) 1 (pg.16)

M2) (I.i.65) quin = quinone; sweet is quin = the pleasures of an achievement is bitter. (<1) 1

M3) (I.i.71) nobuild = not a single person; lark = a person who wakes up early. (<2) (pg.17)

M4) The use of Tilde or ~ means stating or stated by; e.g.
(I.i.78) Whereat salubrious living ~ my glory = my prime need is to live healthily. (<2)

M5) (I.i.81) made above crude = off-limit (<2)

M6) (I.i.93) Without of = Beyond (<3) (pg.18)

M7) (I.i.94) Purlieus of sordidness = desolated surroundings (<3)

M8) (I.i.98) Garner all hope; earn glowed life = there may be a chance when there is a strong hope (<3)

M9) (I.ii.9) Boost the good = Tell the truth (<4) (pg.19)

M10) (I.ii.15-17) noun replace adjective – like cheerless, insalubrious (<5) (pg.20)

M11) (I.ii.22) hefty hurdle = big/serious problem (<5)

M12) (I.ii.24 & 25) fluid truly story = clear statement; additions = fabrication (<5)

M13) (I.ii.26) arear = from behind (<6)

M14) (I.ii.39-40) Acceptance; part kindliness ties = Even no reward, it is still a good deed. (<6) (pg.21)

M15) (I.ii.44) alying the back = unconscious at the rear seat. (<6)

M16) (I.ii.47 & 50) pates = heads; vain folks of gentrification = people who have transformed themselves to rich individuals. (<7) (pg.22)

M17) (I.ii.63) queer street = poor & homeless. (<7)

M18) (I.iii.1) Playing to the gallery = act in an exaggerated way in order to appeal; ayely = always (I.iii.2) (<8) (pg.23)

M19) (I.iii.43) thy primrose the mainspring = pursuit for pleasure as your motivation (<9) (pg.26)

M20) (I.iii.64) latency = still new and unknowing. (<10) (pg.27)

M21) (I.iii.75) time immemorial = long time ago that I could not remember. (<11) (pg.28)

M22) (I.iii.81) brings me not on edge = something that not troubles me. (<11)

M23) (I.iii.86) 'Head = Ahead; oft-fully in credibility = trustworthy at all time/loyal (<11)

M24) (I.iii.98) My uncouthly establishment = I am wild and discourteous (<12) (pg.29)

M25) (I.iii.126) Thee me a trifle actively = You and I actively frivolous. (<13) (pg.30)

M26) (I.iv.15) clop = to sit heavily and fart (perhaps) (<14) (pg.33)

M27) (I.iv.31) min'bus = minibus (a public transport in Kuala Lumpur which were famous in the 80's) (<15)

M28) (I.iv.33) Apeak hours to th' city—non-trippery = It's not fun for excursion during busy office hours. (<15) (pg.34)

M29) (I.v.9) In grip! = Oh gosh! (<16) (pg.35)

M30) (I.v.12) least picked = less resort (<16)

M31) (I.v.32) His additional pleasure; naught kernel = nothing of his other likings is considered important (<17) (pg.36)

ACT II

M32) (II.ia.2) Glory's foamed = I have another success. (<18) (pg.37)

M33) (II.ia.8 & 9) Naught err'd with my part, = It is not my mistake; period's shrunk to expatiate = time is so short to detail my doing. (<18)

M34) (II.ia.18) they are levelled cold = the dishes turns cold. (<18)

M35) (II.ia.26) paean paean! = It's a glory! (<19) (pg.38)

M36) (II.ia.31-32) 'Bove = Above; the revolution of the rack is sketching apacely = the cloud is moving faster and growing bigger. (<19)

M37) (II.ia.45) ravished thus = thus fill me with intense delight.(<20) (pg.40)

M38) (II.ia.54) Myriads of muzzy blunder galant intruding = A lots of indistinct mistakes made by changes in the style of living. (<20)

M39) (II.ib.72) 'Tis all a skit-stir = It is all just to prompt a short joke. (<21) (pg.42)

M40) (II.ib.76 & 77) Lapdog a loser by grace build a balm = a controlled individual though keeps losing still worths a help/ helping hand; the kisser lush a diamond spray = their mouths still speak valuable words. (<21)

M41) (II.ib.81) deep of reverie = a sea of daydream. (<21)

M42) (II.ib.85) A toil beyond lousy = a useless labour. (<21)

M43) (II.ib.90) thou facest the sod. = you may face death. (<22) (pg.43)

M44) (II.ib.par.11) knee-length bags = short loose-fitting trousers. (<22)

M45) (II.ib.96) diet, irrelevent = no means for diet. (<22)

M46) (II.ib.105) Thirsty pace but a delight in its entirety = Fast getting thirsty but the dish is flavoursome. (<23) (pg.44)

M47) (II.ic.113) a lame dog her quiver = her state of pain is awful. (<24) (pg.45)

M48) (II.ic.132) Instinctivable, grace we should repay = Promptly with good will we have to return the kindness. (<25) (pg.46)

M49) (II.ic.135) For thou livest in bourn o' nay sibling e'er = Because you have no brother nor sister before. (<25)

M50) (II.iia.39) fungoid fur = clog by fungus <u>or</u> ailed by disease (<26) (pg.49)

M51) (II.iia.47-48) as well meetly lifting them to a Romano = like properly cure them to be healthy and strong. Romano = strong and healthy man. (<26)

M52) (II.iia.69) kills the cipher's taste = end the bitterness (<27) (pg.50)

M53) (II.iia.95) prayed = pleased (to) (<28) (pg.52)

M54) (II.iib.121) I view a bone man, not sore with his shudder = Even a thin man also is not as nervous as this. (<29) (pg.54)

M55) (II.iiia.9 & 11) outré pecuniary gain = a monetary gain that is (<30) unusual; gaily to graze = enjoy to touch and use. (pp.57-58)

M56) (II.iiia.28) menu = command (<31)

M57) (II.iv.42) doeth thou list hearken = do you like to listen(<32)(pg.63)

M58) (II.iv.44&45) art thou even rejuvenated limning = are you healthy enough to depict (<32)

M59) (II.iv.53) imbroglio = a difficulty (<33) (pg.64)

M60) (II.iv.61) But a substantial asset for anon promotion = a great opportunity for future preferment. (<33)

ACT III

M61) (III.i.1-2) goofy fashions = foolish manners; fiendish sickness = savage disease (<34) (pg.65)

M62) (III.i.6) he's gaudily for my perception = he is not my type. (<34)

M63) (III.i.15) mould = my distinctive character as taught and practised (<35) (pg.66)

M64) (III.i.92) the cloud = the problem (<36) (pg.70)

M65) (III.i.95) And full inebriated for on alcohol influence = totally drunk because of over assumption of alcohol (<36)

M66) (III.i.110) Invalidated their professionalism = their skills that are against the law (<37) (pg.71)

M67) (III.i.111) Th' harsh-entreat'd but beneficial elk's meat = though it seems unjust but gives advantage. (<37)

M68) (III.i.139&140) to nod = that is me; effort a mount = to great effort (<38) (pg.72)

M69) (III.iia.4) With mainstay = with someone you can rely on (<39) (pg.74)

M70) (III.iia.15) I shall examine my sweat = I shall work in this undertaking. (<40) (pg.75)

M71) (III.iia.24) Thou'rt indistinguished being such laggard = You'll not be tolerated for being slow and with low justification. (<40)

M72) (III.iia.27) spry witnesses = live witnesses that besides the accused. (<41) (pg.76)

M73) (III.iia.33) Pray propound thine angle = Please put forward your reasons. (<41)

M74) (III.iib.50) toilet shape = shameless person (<42) (pg.77)

M75) (III.iib.58&59) buttress of lewdness = my vulgar standing; 'way = away. (<42)

M76) (III.iib.74) muddled be = futile be (<43) (pg.78)

M77) (III.iic.1) mates of cur = contemptible friends (<43)

M78) (III.iid.34) in gleam glen and glee = in short delight. (<44) (pg.80)

M79) (III.iid.38) duchess = a seducer (<45) (pg.81)

M80) (III.iie.49&50) facsimile genuine secondaries = a copy of minor (<46) importances which is not strong enough to defend. (pg.82)

M81) (III.iie.57&61) yestermorn = yesterday morning;
'Cause = Because (<46)

M82) (III.iie.70) accused's = accused was; 'mount = amount (<47) (pg.83)

M83) (III.iii.5) thru' = through (<48) (pg.84)

M84) (III.iii.18) Naught but gunning an insidious getter = Nothing else but acting as a malefactor. (<49) (pg.85)

M85) (III.iii.62&66) For he is unfound to disport himself = Because he never frolics; yon = that man (<50) (pg.88)

M86) (III.iv.3) Appreciation along the Jalan Sultan Ismail (<51) (pg.91)

M87) (III.iv.16&17) phased prediliction in the haze = someone that's gradually becoming special in the midst of confusing problem. (<52) (pg.92)

M88) (III.iv.42) heavy-laden romps' rote / rote of romps = the (<53) habitual learning by mistakes of a rough player (pg.93)

M89) (III.iv.46) fresh firmly = absolutely new (<54) (pg.94)

M90) (III.iv.73) love expectant = expectant love (<55) (pg.95)

M91) (III.va.8) th' 'stant = the constant (<56) (pg.98)

M92) (III.va.23) lewd dominion = offensive control or I can easily rape her. (<57) (pg.99)

M93) (III.vb.10) a memory's agape = a surprise from memory(<58)(pg.102)

M94) (III.vb.12) s'pine = supine (<58)

M95) (III.vb.31) Bland with a baloney = Boring with a foolish talk. (<59) (pg.104)

M96) (III.vb.33) Relax the awry bone or marred by gloated globe = Don't feel guilty or your guilt shall ruin you. (<59)

M97) (III.vc.23) What's thy respect with the peevish matter? = (<60) What do you regard about the annoying problem? (pg.106)

M98) (III.vi.6&7) 'normous = enormous; e'nobles = ennobles (<61) (pg.107)

M99) (III.vi.59) By and by ardour departured malady abode = Gradually the enthusiasm recedes and is replaced by sickness. (<62) (pg.110)

M100)(III.vi.94&95) 'Cme = Acme; 'Cquaint'd = Acquainted (<63) (pg.113)

M101)(III.vi.96) Immat'rial put to imb'cile = Being a spirit is just like a stupid dumb. (<63)

M102)(III.vi.104) Plumage materialises the shape's course = Bird's feathers appear and cover throughout the body (<63)

M103)(III.vi.106) time is pursed = time is shortened (<63)

ACT IV

M104) (IV.i.19) chagriner (from French) = rough skin man; personal's bough = main news in newspapers(<64)(pg.120)

M105) (IV.i.20-23) sole capitalist = the most revered and rich investor; iron hot of substance = addicted to drugs; irrationalist = absurd (<64)

M106) (IV.i.26) slump turns poverty = substantial failure in shareholding led him to be totally poor. (<65) (pg.121)

M107) (IV.i.36) captive don't by deploration = imprisoned never by sadness. (<65)

M108) (IV.i.60) Ruritanian pleasure = heavenly situation (<66) (pg.122)

M109) (IV.i.68) Vulnerable is not a sturdy standing = Disability can be ruining especially by the disease anorexia (<67) (pg.123)

M110) (IV.i.76) I'm bathed by my acme of assumption = I am joyful that what I assume is true. (<68) (pg.124)

M111) (IV.i.82-83) thriving with thine excitement not = do not be too joyful (<68)

M112) (IV.i.94) M.S.C. = Multimedia Super Corridor (Malaysia) (<69) (pg.125)

M113) (IV.i.114) distress' pile/ pile of distress = heavy problem (<70) (pg.126)

M114) (IV.i.131-132) I'm without anomaly mother's waft = I am unsuitable even a while to be a mother to animals. (<71) (pg.127)

M115) (IV.iia.7-8) Haven't conjectured my configuration? = Still not remember my appearance? (<72) (pg.128)

M116) (IV.iia.24) Six moons till this triumph = Six months until this gainful moment. (<73) (pg.129)

M117) (IV.iia.66) frame of thought = mind (<74) (pg.131)

M118) (IV.iib.125) mock-up lurked / lurked mock-up = not to be a noticeable piece of experiment. (<75) (pg.135)

M119) (IV.iib.174) I'm shifting without my conceit = I am outside of my notion/perception (<76) (pg.138)

M120) (IV.iic.180) cryptic excrescence = secret peril (<76)

M121) (IV.iic.182) quick bones = liveliness (<77) (pg.139)

M122) (IV.iic.185) a quirk of natural revolution = a chance of either live or death. (<77)

M123) (IV.iii.12) Moping maximal with Olan's kismet = Olan's destiny is further worsened. (<78) (pg.141)

M124) (IV.iii.29) blood star = terrible happening (<79) (pg.142)

M125)	(IV.iv.1)	By stages = step by step (<80)	(pg.143)
M126)	(IV.v)	(<81)	
M127)	(IV.vi)	(<82)	
M128)	(IV.vii.33)	My stability is vitiated; bowed spirit = my (<83) stability is impaired and my soul is down.	(pg.161)

ACT V

M129)	(V.i.4)	accuracy pure = exactly (<84)	(pg.167)
M130)	(V.i.5)	irrepressibly = straightforward (<84)	
M131)	(V.i.9)	I'm a trifle flummox'd with an ill watch = I am a little bewildered to peek. (<84)	
M132)	(V.i.16)	M.S. = Master of Science (<84)	
M133)	(V.ii.8)	fatuous Graces or foolish Graces = agitator (<85)	(pg.170)
M134)	(V.ii.14)	discordant tumour = never ending squabble (<85)	
M135)	(V.ii.15)	a tumble or fall = over (<85)	
M136)	(V.ii.16)	swelling liking = love very much (<85)	
M137)	(V.ii.18)	I'm a stoic = I become a person that can endure troubles and hardship (<85)	
M138)	(V.ii.23)	Hard by my hankering = I really want to know and visit (instead of 'have'; because a grave cannot be owned) (<85)	
M139)	(V.ii.24)	I would frame a circuit = I would mind-map (<85)	
M140)	(V.ii.31)	In thy category = to your choice? Which means you want us to use your Tiara car? [Tiara = Proton Tiara; Malaysian supermini hatchback] (<86)	(pg.171)
M141)	(V.ii.41-42)	Wagging first pulse of debt—the publicity = Your being indebted to me shall be published in the newspapers. (<86)	
M142)	(V.ii.49)	favourite's prime = main choice. (<87)	(pg.172)
		Note: [V.ii.36-51] Nixloath is angry with Antidoubt for joking about the eagle, by which is their real father. And Nixloath warns Antidoubt to treat the eagle as a respectable object.	
M143)	(V.ii.57)	Thine odour shifts my knifed primness away = Your perfume throws away my bad mood (because of being scolded by Nixloath) (<87)	

M144)	(V.ii.63&64)	when the moment is in its mellowness (humor) = when time permits; Thou shalt befriend the gold favour = You will get the present. (<88)	(pg.173)
M145)	(V.iii.3)	I'm modish to my perennial muddle = I'm getting forgetful (<89)	(pg.174)
M146)	(V.iii.6)	a fused timepiece = wristwatch not working	
M147)	(V.iii.15)	a parcel by a whisker = a small gift (<89)	
M148)	(V.iii.16)	a jocose brush = a touch of playfulness <u>or</u> a short humor. (<89)	
M149)	(V.iii.46)	Thou'rt pitched for bone = You are getting thinner; Pinch the pity and work some for thyself = Don't diet because of financial inconvenience but rather try better provision. (<90)	(pg.176)
M150)	(V.iii.60)	Patent banter = It is obvious a joke (<91)	(pg.177)
M151)	(V.iii.73)	Recurrent nay = Always not <u>or</u> Never will; Recalcitrant = Obstinately reluctant (<92)	(pg.178)
M152)	(V.iii.88)	a main in staunch kinship = a great importance in loyal relationship. (<93)	(pg.180)
M153)	(V.iii.106)	sated = satisfied (<94)	(pg.181)
M154)	(V.iii.108)	spurs = incentives (<94)	

www.ingramcontent.com/pod-product-compliance
Lightning Source LLC
Chambersburg PA
CBHW071743150726
47998CB00005B/1775
* 9 7 8 9 6 7 2 6 6 3 9 0 4 *